"I'd really like to see you again," Cameron said.

Snap! Rosie's eyes flew north till they met his. Deep, blue, heaven… "Seriously?"

He laughed. She bit her lip.

Just because he'd used her full name in such a deferential way, and just because more than once she'd caught him looking at her as if she was the most fascinating creature on the planet, it didn't mean she should go forgetting herself.

He said, "Do you want a list of reasons why? Or would you prefer them in the form of a poem?"

Rosie's heart danced. She knew that taking guidance from one's heart was as sensible as using one's liver for financial-planning advice, having witnessed firsthand what listening to the dancing of your heart could do to a woman. If she needed any further reason to call it a day…

And then Cameron had to go and say, "What are you doing tomorrow?"

Dear Reader,

Did you know that this year is Harlequin's sixtieth birthday? Well, it is!

Thinking about it takes me back to the much-loved dog-eared favorites my grandmother kept in boxes galore under her spare bed. I can still smell the old paper, see the creased, faded covers of books read and reread by a true fan and remember opening book after book to check if I had read the story before. And then came a new opening line, a new first time a heroine saw her hero and an old familiar rush of anticipation, delight and warmth.

To tell you the truth, not much has changed! Okay, so maybe a little. The Harlequin books I read now I have picked up in bookstores, not from under my grandmother's bed. Many of them are now written by wonderful, wise, warm women I consider friends. And I am absolutely honored to be a writer of Harlequin romance novels myself. But in the reading, that old familiar feeling that sneaks up when I sink into a story has never gone away.

The very idea that, out there in the world, a reader might pick up one of my books, read the first line and settle in, knowing that she will be in for a fun, flirtatious, moving, sigh-filled ride amazes me every day.

So thanks, Harlequin, for letting me be a part of your world, then and now. Happy birthday and many happy returns!

Ally

www.allyblake.com

ALLY BLAKE

Dating the Rebel Tycoon

TORONTO • NEW YORK • LONDON
AMSTERDAM • PARIS • SYDNEY • HAMBURG
STOCKHOLM • ATHENS • TOKYO • MILAN • MADRID
PRAGUE • WARSAW • BUDAPEST • AUCKLAND

Recycling programs
for this product may
not exist in your area.

ISBN-13: 978-0-373-17599-4

DATING THE REBEL TYCOON

First North American Publication 2009.

Copyright © 2009 by Ally Blake.

Having once been a professional cheerleader, **Ally Blake** has a motto: "Smile and the world smiles with you." One way to make Ally smile is by sending her on holidays—especially to locations that inspire her writing. New York and Italy are by far her favorite destinations. Other things that make her smile are the gracious city of Melbourne, the gritty Collingwood football team and her gorgeous husband, Mark.

Reading romance novels was a smile-worthy pursuit from long back, so with such valuable preparation already behind her she wrote and sold her first book. Her career as a writer also gives her a perfectly reasonable excuse to indulge in her stationery addiction. That alone is enough to keep her grinning every day!

Ally would love for you to visit her at her Web site, www.allyblake.com.

Ally also writes for Harlequin Presents®!

To my baby Boo.
You own my heart, you crack me up,
you dazzle me daily,
and it is my absolute privilege
watching you become you.
Love Mum xxx

CHAPTER ONE

CAMERON Kelly opened the heavy side-door of the random building, shut it smartly behind him and became enveloped in darkness. The kind of inky darkness that would make even the bravest boy imagine monsters under the bed.

It was some years since Cameron had been a boy, longer still since he'd realised people didn't always tell the truth. When he'd found out his two older brothers had made the monsters up.

The small window between himself and the Brisbane winter sunshine outside revealed the coast was clear, and he let his forehead rest on the cold glass with a sheepish *thunk*.

Of all the people he could have seen—many miles from where a man such as he ought to have been while commerce and industry raged on in the city beyond—it had to have been his younger sister Meg, downing take-away coffee and gabbing with her girlfriends.

If Meg had seen him wandering the suburban Botanical Gardens, pondering lily pads and cacti rather than neck-deep in blueprints and permits and funding for multi-million-dollar sky-scrapers, she would not have let him be until he'd told her why.

So he, a grown man—a man of means, and most of the time sense—was hiding. Because the truth would only hurt her. And, even though he'd long since been cast as the black sheep of the Kelly clan, hurting those he cared about was the last thing he would ever intentionally do.

He held his watch up to the parcel of light, saw it was nearly nine and grimaced.

Hamish and Bruce, respectively his architect and his project manager, would have been at the CK Square site for more than an hour waiting for him to approve the final plans for the fifty-fourth floor. This close to the end of a very long job, if they hadn't throttled one another by now then he would be very lucky.

He made to open the door to leave, remembered Meg—the one person whose leg he'd never been able to pull, even with two adept older brothers to show him how—and was over-taken by a stronger compulsion than the desire to play inter-mediary between two grown men. His hand dropped.

Let the boys think he was making a grand entrance when he finally got there. It'd give them something to agree upon for once. He could live with people thinking he had an ego the size of Queensland. He was a Kelly, after all; impressions of grandeur came with the name.

'We're closed,' a voice echoed somewhere behind him.

He spun on his heel, hairs on the back of his neck standing on end. Though he hadn't boxed since his last year at St Grellans, in a flash his fists were raised, his fingers wrapped so tight around his thumbs they creaked. Lactic acid burned in his arms. It seemed fresh air, sunshine and tiptoeing through the tulips weren't the catharsis for an uneasy mind that they were cracked up to be.

He peered around the huge empty space and couldn't see a thing past the end of his nose, bar a square of pink burned into his retina from the bright light of the window.

'I'm desperately sorry,' the voice said. 'I seem to have given you a little fright.'

Unquestionably female, it was, husky, sweet, mellow tones drifting to him through the darkness with a surprisingly vivid dash of sarcasm, considering she had no idea who she was dealing with.

'You didn't frighten me,' he insisted.

'Then how about you put down your dukes before you knock yourself out?'

Cameron, surprised to find his fists were still raised, unclenched all over, letting his hands fall to his sides before shucking his blazer back onto his shoulders.

'Now, I love an eager patron as much as the next gal,' the mocking voice said. 'But the show doesn't start for another half-hour. Best you wait outside.'

The show? Cameron's eyes had become more used to the light, or lack thereof. He could make out a bumpy outline on the horizon, rows of seats decked out auditorium-style. They tipped backwards slightly so that an audience could look upwards without getting neck strain, as the show that went on in this place didn't happen on stage but in the massive domed sky above.

He'd stumbled into the planetarium.

Wow. He hadn't been in the place since he was a kid. It seemed the plastic bucket seats and industrial carpet scraping beneath his shoes hadn't changed.

He craned his neck back as far as it would go, trying to make out the shape and form of the roof. The structural engineer in him wondered about the support mechanisms for the high ceiling, while the vestiges of the young boy who'd once upon a time believed in monsters under the bed simply marvelled at the deep, dark, infinite black.

Finally, thankfully, one thing or another managed to shake loose a measure of the foreboding that ruminating over rhododendrons had not.

He kept looking up as he said, 'I'll wait, if it's alright by you.'

'Actually, it's not.'

'Why not?'

'Rules. Regulations. Occupational health and safety. Fire hazards. Today's Tuesday. You're wearing the wrong shoes. Take your pick.'

He slowly lowered his head, glancing down at his perfectly

fine shoes, which he could barely see, and he was a heck of a lot closer to them than she was.

He peered back out into the nothingness, but still he couldn't make her out—whoever she was.

Was she security, ready to throw him out on his ear? A fellow interloper protecting her find? A delusion, born out of an acute desire to change the subject that had shanghaied his thoughts since he'd caught the financial news on TV that morning?

'Go now, and I can reserve you a seat,' the honeyed tones suggested.

Management, then. And strangely anticlimactic.

'I'll even personally find you a nice, comfy seat,' she continued. 'Smack bang in the centre, with no wobbles or lumps, that doesn't squeak every time you ooh or aah at the show. What do you say?'

He didn't say anything. He could tell she'd moved closer by a slight shifting of the air to his left, the sound of cloth whispering against skin, and the sudden sweet scent of vanilla making his stomach clench with hunger.

Had he forgotten to eat breakfast? Yes, he had. He swore softly as he remembered why.

The appearance on the financial report on the TV news by the very man who had made him a family outcast many years before had not been a bolt from the blue. Quinn Kelly, his father, was a shameless self-promoter of the family business: the Kelly Investment Group, or 'KInG' as it was irresistibly dubbed in the press.

His father was the epitome of the Australian dream. An immigrant who had come to the country as a boy with nothing to his name but the clothes on his back, he had built himself the kind of large, rambunctious, photogenic family the press prized, and a financial empire men envied. Tall, handsome, charming, straight-talking, the man acted as though he would live for ever, and the world believed him—needed to believe him—because he had his fingers in so many financial pies.

Cameron hadn't realised he'd believed the man to be immortal too until he'd noticed the pallor make-up couldn't hide, the weight lost from his cheeks, the dullness in his usually sharp eyes that would only have been noticed by someone who went out of his way not to catch a glimpse of the man every day.

For that reason it was highly possible that not even the family knew something was very wrong with Quinn Kelly. The rest of the clan was so deeply a part of one another's lives he could only imagine they had not noticed the infinitesimal changes.

He'd lost hours trying to convince himself it wasn't true. And not for the kinds of reasons that made him a good son, but because he'd felt the sharp awakening of care for a man not worth caring about. Why should he care for a man who'd so blithely severed him from his family to save his own hide, and that was after laying waste to any naivety Cameron might have yet possessed about loyalty and fidelity? And at an age when he'd not even had a chance to make those decisions himself.

It wasn't even nine in the morning and already Cameron wished this day was well and truly over.

'The door is right behind you,' the only highlight in his day so far said.

Cameron pulled himself up to his full height in the hope the unwanted concerns might run off his back. 'While I'm enjoying the thought of you testing each and every seat for me, I'm not here to see the show.'

'You don't have to act coy with me,' she said, her teasing voice lifting him until he felt himself rocking forward on his toes. 'Even big boys like you have been known to find comfort in the idea that there might be something bigger and grander than you are, out there in the cosmos, that will burn bright long after you are a two-line obituary in your local paper.'

Surprising himself, he laughed out loud, something he had not expected to do today. It wasn't often people dared to tease him. He was too successful, his reputation too implacable, his surname too synonymous with winning at all costs. Perhaps that was why he liked it.

'Your expertise on the ways of big boys aside,' he said, 'I saw the show years ago in middle school.'

'Years ago?' the husky voice lobbed back. 'Lucky for you, astronomers hit a point at *exactly* that point in time when they said, "Well, that'll do us. We've found enough stars out there for a hundred generations of couples to name after one another for Valentine's Day. Why bother studying the eternal mystery of the universe any more?"'

He laughed again. And for the first time in hours he felt like he could turn his neck without fear of pulling a muscle. He had not a clue if the woman was eighteen or eighty, if she was married or single, or even from this planet, but he was enjoying himself too much to care.

He took a step away from the door. He couldn't see the floor beneath his feet. It felt liberating, like he was stepping out into an abyss.

Until he stubbed his toe, and then it felt like he was walking around in a strange building in the dark.

Something moved. Cameron turned his head a fraction to the left, and finally he saw her: a dark blob melting into the shadows. If she was standing on the same level as him, she was tall. There was a distinct possibility of long, wavy hair, and lean curves poured into a floaty calf-length dress. When he imagined seriously chunky boots, he realised he didn't have any kind of perspective to trust his eyes.

But he'd always trusted his gut. And, while he'd come to the gardens searching for the means to navigate his way around a difficult truth, the only real truth he had so far found was the voice tugging him further into the blackness.

'How about you turn on a light?' he said. 'Then we can come to an arrangement that suits us both.'

'Would you believe I'm conserving power?'

There wasn't a single thing about the tone of her voice that made him even half believe her. His smile became a grin, and the tightness in his shoulders just melted away.

He took another step.

'Not for even half a second,' he said, his voice dropping several notes, giving as good as he got to that voice—that husky, feminine voice. Mocking him. Taking him down a peg or two. Or three, if he was at all honest.

He—a Kelly and all.

Rosie kept her distance.

Not because the intruder seemed all that dangerous; she knew the nooks and crannies of this place like the back of her hand, and after stargazing half her life she could see in the dark as well as a cat. And from the lazy way he'd held his fists earlier, like he'd instinctively known nobody would dare take a swipe, she'd surely have been able to get in a jab or two.

She kept her distance because she knew exactly who he was.

The man in the dark jeans, pinstriped blazer, glossy tie and crisp chambray shirt poking out at the bottom of the kind of knit V-necked vest only the most super-swanky guy could get away with was Cameron Kelly.

Too-beautiful-for-words Cameron Kelly. Smart, serious, eyes-as-deep-as-the-ocean Cameron Kelly. Of the Ascot Kellys. The huge family, investment-banking dynasty, lived their lives in the social pages, absolutely blessed in every possible way Kellys.

She would have recognised that untameable cowlick, those invulnerable shoulders, and the yummy creases lining the back of that neck anywhere. God only knew how many hours she'd spent in the St Grellans school chapel staring at them.

Not that getting up close and personal or turning on the light would have rendered her familiar. She'd been the scholarship kid who'd taken two buses and a train to get to school from the indifferent council flat she'd shared with her single mum. He had attended St Grellans by birthright.

Post-school they'd run in very different circles, but the Kellys had never been far from the periphery of her life. The glossy mags had told her that dashing patriarch Quinn Kelly was seen buying this priceless *objet d'art* or selling that racehorse, while his wife Mary was putting on sumptuous banquets for one or another head of state. Brendan, the eldest, and his father's right-hand man, had married, had two beautiful daughters, then become tragically widowed, adding to the family folklore. Dylan, the next in line, was the charmer, his wide, white smile inviting every magazine reader to dare join the bevy of beauties no longer on his speed dial. Meg, the youngest, was branded bored and beautiful enough to rival any Hollywood starlet.

Yet the one Rosie had always had a soft spot for remained mostly absent from the prying eyes of the paparazzi. He'd played into the Kelly legend just enough by sporting fresh new consorts every other week: a fabulous blonde senator on his arm at some party here, a leggy blonde dancer tucked in behind him at a benefit there.

Yet the minute he'd appeared without a blonde in sight, her soft spot had begun to pulse.

'Rightio,' she said, curling away to her left, away from Cameron and towards the bank of stairs leading to the front of the auditorium. 'What are you doing here if not to once and for all find out who truly did hang the moon and the stars?'

'Central heating,' he said without missing a beat. 'It's freezing out there.'

She grinned, all too readily charmed considering the guy still seemed to have blinkers when it came to skinny, smart girls with indefinite hair-colour and no cleavage to speak of.

And now she was close enough to make out the subtle, chequered pattern of his vest, the fine platinum thread through the knot of his tie, and the furrowing of his brow as his eyes almost found hers.

She took two definite steps back. 'The café just up the hill has those cool outdoor furnace-heaters—big, shiny brass ones that have to be seen to be believed. And I hear they also serve coffee, which is a bonus.'

After much longer than was at all polite, his voice drifted to her on a rumble. 'The allure of coffee aside, the warmth in here is more appealing.'

Her knees wobbled. She held out both arms to steady herself. Seriously, how could the guy still manage to incapacitate her knees without trying to, without meaning to? Without even knowing her name.

She wrapped her russet beaded-cardigan tighter around herself, squeezing away the return of an old familiar ache that she thought she'd long since cast off: the sting of growing up invisible.

Growing up with a dad who'd left before she was born, and a mum who'd never got over him, being inconspicuous had come with the territory. Being a shy unfortunate in a school saturated with the progeny of politicians, moguls and even royalty hadn't helped the matter.

But since then she'd achieved a master's degree in astrophysics, run with the bulls, stood at the foot of the sphinx, spent a month on grappa and fresh air on a boat off Venice and surveyed the stars from every corner of the globe. She'd come to terms with where she'd come from. And now hers was a life lived large and not for anyone else to define.

Cameron took another step forward, and she flinched, then indulged in a good eye-roll. An eyelash caught in her contact lens, which was about all she deserved.

As she carefully pulled it free she told herself that, just as she'd evolved, this guy wasn't *that* Cameron Kelly any more— the Cameron Kelly who'd seemed the kind of guy who'd smile back if she'd ever found the pluck to smile first. Maybe he never even had been.

Right now he was the guy wasting the last precious minutes she had with the observatory telescope, before Venus, her bread and butter, disappeared from view.

'Okay, tell it to me straight. What do I have to say or do to get you to vamoose?' She paused to shuffle her contact lens back into place. 'I know Italian, Spanish, a little Chinese. Any chance "off you pop" in any of those languages will make a dent?'

'What if I leave and not another soul turns up?'

Rosie threw her arms out sideways. 'I'll…grab a seat, put my feet up on the chair in front and throw popcorn at the ceiling, while saying all the lines along with the narrator. It wouldn't be the first time.'

That got her another laugh, a deep, dry, rumbling, masculine sort of laugh. Her knees felt it first, then the rest of her joined in, finishing off with her toes curling pleasurably into her socks.

She remembered exactly what the smile that went along with the laugh looked like. Deep brackets around his mouth. Appealing crinkles fanning out from a pair of cornflower-blue eyes. And there was even a dimple thrown in for good measure.

Yikes, she hadn't waded quite so deep into the miasma of her past in a long time. It was time she moved the guy on before he had her remembering former lives.

Knowing he'd follow, she circled him to the left and herded him towards the exit. 'I thought you weren't interested in the show?'

'You should never have told me about the popcorn.'

He edged closer, and she could tell by the slightest amount of diffused light from the window in the door behind her adding colour to his clothes that she couldn't back away much further.

She glanced at the glowing clock on the wall by the ticket office. Venus would only be visible another fifteen minutes at most. If she wanted to finish the day's assessment, she'd have to get cracking. 'So, try a movie. Far more action.'

'More action than supernovas, red dwarfs and meteor showers?'

'You boys and your love of all exploding, fiery things,' she said. 'Thank goodness there are women in the world to appreciate the finer details of the universe. You should sit still and just stare at the moon once in a while. You'd be amazed at the neural pathways a little down-time can open up.'

'Maybe I will.' This time the lift of one blazer-covered shoulder was obvious in the hazy sunlight. 'I was holding out on you before. I have my own telescope.'

Damn it! There weren't many things he could have said to have distracted her, but even a passing interest in the one great overriding passion in her life was a pull she couldn't resist.

'What type?' she asked.

'It's silver. Not solid silver. Maybe not even silver. Silver looking.'

'The silver-look ones are the best. It comes down to the light refracting off all that extra shininess.'

His half-second pause as he decided whether or not she was taking the mickey out of him was a pleasure. So much of a pleasure it made her soft spot for him stretch and purr.

'To tell you the truth,' he said, 'All I remember from way back when is the bit about the wormholes. And I'm man enough to admit I lost a couple of nights' sleep over them.'

His voice was low. Rough. Suggestive. Her bad, bad lungs contracted until the air inside her felt like it had nowhere else to go but out in a great, big fat sigh.

She played with a turquoise bead on her cardigan. It had been sewn by the hand of a woman she'd found on the way to Rosarito, Mexico. She'd lived alone in a shack made of things she'd found on the edge of the most beautiful beach in the entire world. It reminded Rosie that she'd been places, seen amazing things, and was not easily impressed.

Waxing lyrical in the dark with Cameron Kelly ought not to feel so much like a highlight.

She straightened up. 'Fine. Since you're not staying for the show, I'll let you in on the big climax. Pluto isn't a planet any more.'

'It's not?' he asked, genuinely shocked. 'Poor Pluto.'

This time she was the one to laugh. Loose, low and most enjoyable.

And then she realised, all too late, that Cameron was close

enough now that she could see the sunlight brush over evenly tanned skin, a straight nose, a smooth jaw and deep-set eyes. Eyes that had become so used to the light that they'd finally found hers.

He wasn't likely to be able to see much more than their shape, and perhaps the curve where ambiguous grey met the dark edges of her pupils, which were no doubt dilated from the lack of light. But he certainly seemed keen to try.

When his eyes left hers, she breathed again. Unfortunately she was not to be let off so lightly.

His glance took in her hair, which was likely a mess, since she'd had it up, down, twisted in a knot and in plaits since she'd arrived a little before sunrise. Then there was her long, floral dress she'd thrown on that morning because it had been atop the clean-clothes basket, the cardigan she'd found in the back of her car, and the comfortable boots that had taken her all over the world and brought her home again in one piece—but did little in terms of being fashionable or flattering.

It was the briefest of perusals. Really no more than a flick of his gaze. But that didn't stop her from wanting to fix her hair, hitch her bra, and wipe fingers beneath her eyes to remove any traces of smudged mascara that several hours of awake-time would have left behind.

Thankfully his gaze cut back to her eyes.

All traces of thankfulness dried up smartly when those famously blue eyes remained fixed on hers. Her throat grew dry. She tried to swallow, only to find she couldn't quite remember how.

She had the distinct feeling time was running out on something she was meant to be doing, but she couldn't for the life of her remember what it was. She wished ultra-hard for a light-bulb moment.

And got one.

Fluorescent bulbs by the dozen flickered in the walls around them, strobing on and off like disco lights.

In between dark patches, Cameron's eyes locked with hers, deep, dark, determined. She wondered for a moment how she'd ever thought she knew him...

And then he smiled. Cheek brackets. Eye crinkles. Dimple. And she felt like she was fourteen years old, complete with glasses, funny clothes and a crush.

Her glasses had been exchanged for contacts, and her now mostly pre-loved wardrobe was probably still a little funny. But at least the moony kid she'd once been was no more.

With every flash of intense white light, Rosie made sure her feet were well and truly on the ground.

CHAPTER TWO

ADELE, Rosie thought, giving the word in her head all the oomph of a curse.

It had to be Adele who'd turned on the lights. She was Rosie's best friend, the astronomer in residence at the planetarium, the one who let her use the observatory whenever she pleased, and the woman she most wished to tie up and gag most of the time—now being one of those times.

'That puts a whole new spin on "let there be light",' Cameron said, looking around before his gaze landed back on hers.

Even her amazing night-sight wasn't enough to ready her for the true wallop those of eyes: bluer than blue; the bluest blue. Bordered by thick chestnut lashes the same colour as his perfectly scruffy hair.

As for the rest of him...

As tended to be the way of the gods, they had decided that the boy who'd once had it all would turn out even better for the ageing. The years had sharpened the smooth edges, filled out the willing frame and tempered the blazing confidence of youth so that intense self-assurance now wrapped tight around him like a second skin.

Which congruently, in all her loose-haired, comfy-shoed, laid-back glory, made her feel like something the cat had dragged in. She fought the need to rewrap her cardigan tighter again.

'Jeez, hon, you sure you're not becoming a vampire?' Adele

called as she clumped up the stairs. 'All that night-time activity finally getting to you? Oh, sorry. I didn't know you had company.'

Rosie's eyes swept to her friend, who was grinning and raising her eyebrows manically and pointing a thumb at Cameron's back.

Rosie quieted her friend with a withering look as she explained, 'I was just failing miserably at trying to convince this gentleman that we were not yet open and that he ought to come back another time.'

'Cameron,' he said, stepping closer. 'The gentleman's name is Cameron.'

Rosie blinked into his eyes.

It took a second or two before she realised he had stretched out a hand for shaking. She placed her hand in his. Warmth met cool. Soft skin met skin weathered by manual labour.

Her eyes flickered back to his. Manual labour? She searched his eyes for something to answer the unspoken question, but no matter how hard she tried she couldn't see even a millimetre beneath the blue. Because he didn't want her to, or because he didn't want *anyone* to?

Cameron Kelly, clean-cut and preppy, had been yummy. Cameron Kelly with hidden qualities was a force to be reckoned with.

'Rosalind,' Adele called out, leaning her backside against a chair before noisily biting down on an apple. 'The lady's name is Rosalind. Like the eighth moon of Uranus.'

'Like the character from *As You Like It*,' Rosie corrected. 'The eighth moon of Uranus wasn't discovered until 1986.'

'Either way, it's a pleasure to meet you, Rosalind,' Cameron said, somehow making the antiquated name she'd only ever thought of as just another hurdle sound almost wistful, pretty, romantic. She found herself correcting her posture to match.

Then she realised that, even with her name attached, there was still not a glimmer of recognition in the cool depths of his gaze.

She quickly deflated back into her normal, regular, perfectly content self. She did not need any man to notice her in order to feel interesting—and she couldn't believe she was really having to remind herself of that.

Then Cameron said, 'I realise this sounds incredibly corny, but have we met?'

'Smooth,' Adele muttered from the sidelines.

Rosie shot her so-called friend a frosty glare, but Adele only pointed at her watch, meaning they were about to open to the public.

Knowing that to pretend she had no idea what he was on about would only make her feel even more foolish, Rosie said, 'We have. I'm Rosie Harper. I was below you at St Grellans. I took advanced maths with Dr Blackman the same time as you.'

The fact that she'd spent more time imagining what it might be like to kiss him than taking actual notes had led to a B- that had threatened her full academic scholarship.

It had been a watershed moment; proving she'd inherited her mother's propensity to fall hard, and indiscriminately, and with no thought of self-protection.

She now protected herself so vigorously, even the common cold had a hard time getting near.

'Small world,' Cameron finally said, almost hiding the fact that he still couldn't place her behind the charming, crinkle-eyed, dimpled smile that had likely got him out of trouble his whole life.

His hand moulded ever so slightly more snugly around hers. She'd forgotten they were still holding hands, while he held on with a purpose she was only now just beginning to fathom.

His smile warmed, deepened, drew her in, as he said, 'In the interests of remaining corny, what do you say we—?'

The door behind him slammed open before he got out another word, and a harried-looking woman burst inside.

Rosie sprang away from Cameron as though they'd been two teenagers caught *in flagrante*. She ran the hand he'd been holding across the back of her hot neck, only to find the hand was hotter still.

The anxious woman said, 'Sorry to intrude. I'm Miss Granger, Kenmore South grade-four class teacher. Please tell me I can send the kids in? Another minute in the open and they'll be beyond my control.'

The teacher somehow managed to smile through her stress. Probably because she directed her comments entirely towards Cameron, who did look more in charge in his blazer and tie than Rosie did in her vintage get-up—and that was putting a nice spin on it.

Or maybe it was that indefinable X-factor that meant every woman he ever encountered ended up inexorably spinning in his orbit. Rosie, it seemed, was destined to be within perilously close proximity to this particular heavenly body once every fifteen or so years.

Fifteen years earlier he'd been a beautiful boy who'd brushed shoulders with her once or twice in a crowd. This time round he was a fully grown man who saw something in her that made him rethink moving on just yet. She'd hate to think what another fifteen years might do to the man's potency. Or aim.

She glanced up after a good few seconds staring at his shoulders to find him watching her. Unblinking. Radiating authority and curiosity.

Break eye contact, her inner voice said; *back away, roll into the foetal position, whatever it takes to make him head back to his side of the street leaving you to yours.*

'Pretty please?' the teacher asked Cameron.

Rosie had a feeling the woman was asking a completely different question from her first.

Before Rosie had the chance to tell Miss Granger she was barking up the wrong man, Adele called out, 'Send 'em on in, hon! Who are we to turn away those ready and raring to learn about the mysteries of the universe?'

'Who indeed?' Cameron asked.

Rosie steadfastly ignored him and his rumbling voice as Miss Granger heaved the heavy side door-open again, letting in wisps of cool late-winter air and a throng of kids in green tartan school uniforms, half-mast beige socks and floppy wide-brimmed hats.

They slid into the arena like water spurting through a bottle neck. But at the first sign of a break Cameron slipped through until he stood beside Rosie, well and truly within her personal space.

She kept her eyes dead ahead, but couldn't ignore the tug of his gravitational pull, the scent of new cotton, winter, and clean male skin. She breathed in deep through her nose, then pinched the soft part of her hand between her thumb and her index finger in punishment.

'Any feet seen touching any chairs will be forcibly removed!' Adele said as she was carried away with the noisy crowd.

And all too soon it was just the two of them again. Alone, in the unforgiving fluorescent light that couldn't seem to find one bad angle on him.

'It seems you really do have to get to work,' Cameron said, a hint of something that sounded a heck of a lot like the dashing of hope tinging his words.

Rosie's heart twitched, and kept on twitching. She coughed hard, and it found its regular steady pattern once more.

'No rest for the wicked,' she said, turning to him, thus allowing herself one last look before she brought this strange encounter to a halt.

Looking was allowed. Looking at pretty, bright, hot things was her job. And as it was much safer doing so from a great distance she began backing away, thus setting in motion the next fifteen years until they crossed paths again.

'It was great seeing you again, Rosalind.' A glint lit eyes that she was entirely sure had been that exact cornflower-blue from the moment he'd been born.

A jaunty salute and she was gone, hitting the top step at a

jog and not stopping until she reached the control room at the bottom, as from there she couldn't tell if he had turned and left or if he'd watched her walk away.

The outer door shut behind Cameron with a clang, sending him out into the cold over-bright morning.

He stood on one spot for a good thirty seconds, letting the winter sun beat down upon his face, savouring the pleasant, hazy blur that an encounter with an intriguing woman could induce.

Rosalind Harper. St Grellans alumnus. How had he managed to go through the same school without once noticing that soft, pale skin, those temptingly upturned lips that just begged to be teased into a smile and the kind of mussed, burnished waves that made a man just want to reach out and touch?

He took a deep breath through his nose and glanced at his watch. What he saw there brought him back down to earth. And lower still.

Into his father's world.

Quinn Kelly was a shameless, selfish shark who a long time ago had convinced Cameron to keep a terrible secret to keep his family from being torn apart.

He'd done so the only way he'd known how, cutting himself off from the family business. As he saw it, if the man was as unscrupulous in his business dealings as he was in his personal life, God help the stock holders. Quinn on the other hand had seen it as a greater betrayal, and had cut him off completely, which in the end made for a nice cover as to why the two of them couldn't be in the same room together.

It hadn't for a minute been easy, looking his mother, brothers and sister in the eye while knowing what they did not. In the end he'd worked day and night to establish his own career, his own identity, his own manic pace with nonexistent down-time in which to miss those things he no longer had, or yearn for things he'd learnt the hard way didn't really exist, or scratch himself, giving himself a reasonable excuse to decline attendance at enough family gatherings that it was now simply assumed he would not come.

There was the rub. There was no subtle way to sound the others out. The only way to know for sure was to ask the man himself.

The opportunity was there, winking at him like a great cosmic joke. His father's seventieth birthday was less than a week away, and that was one invitation he had not managed to avoid. Every member of his family had called to remind him, all bar the big man himself.

There was no way he'd attend. For if it gave that man even an inkling that deep down he still gave a damn…

The echo of a bombastic musical-score sprang up inside the domed building behind him, more than matching the clashing inside his head. The star show had begun.

Cameron looked to his watch again. It didn't give him any better news. He shoved his hands deep into his trouser pockets, turned up the collar of his jacket against the cold and jogged towards the car park, the diminishing crunch of pine leaves beneath his feet taking him further and further from the gardens.

He turned to watch the great white dome of the planetarium peek through the canopy of gum trees. Quite the handy distraction he'd found himself back there. With her sharp tongue and raw, unassuming sex-appeal, Rosalind Harper had made him forget both work and family for as long a while as he could remember doing in one hit in quite some time.

He hit the car park, picked out his MG, vaulted into the driver's seat, revved the engine and took off through the mostly empty car park, following the scents of smog, car exhaust, money and progress as he headed towards the central business district of the river city.

And the further away he got from all that fresh air and clear open sky—and from Rosalind Harper, her bedroom hair and straightforward playfulness—the heavier he felt the weight bear down upon his shoulders once again.

The fact that she was still at the forefront of his mind five sets of traffic lights later didn't mean he'd gone soft. It simply wasn't in his make-up to do so.

His parents had been married nearly fifty years. They were touted throughout the land as one of the great enduring romances of the modern age. Such tales had filled newspaper and magazine columns, and at one time they'd even had a tele-movie made about them.

But, if the specifics of their marriage was as good as it could get, he wasn't buying. Even a relationship that to the world looked to be secure, long-lasting, deeply committed could be a sham. What was the point?

The short-term company of an easygoing, uncomplicated woman, on the other hand, could work wonders. A dalliance with the promise of no promises. Having the end plan on the table before the project began sat very comfortably with the engineer in him.

Rosalind Harper had been an excellent distraction, and he knew enough to know that behind the impudent exterior she hadn't been completely immune to him. The spark had sparked both ways.

He saw a gap in the traffic, changed down a gear and roared into the spot.

His stomach lifted and fell with the hills of Milton Road, and he realised if he was going to endure the next week with any semblance of ease a distraction was exactly what he needed.

That afternoon, after taking a nap to make up for her usual pre-dawn start to the day, Rosie sat on the corrugated metal step of her digs: a one-bed, one-bath, second-hand caravan.

As she sipped a cooling cup of coffee, she stared unseeingly at the glorious hectare of Australian soil she owned overlooking the Samford Valley, a neat twenty-five-minute drive from the city.

For a girl who'd been happy to travel for many a year, the second she'd seen the spot she'd fallen for it. The gently undu-lating parcel of land had remained verdant through the drought by way of a fat, rocky stream slicing through a gully at the rear. High grass covered the rest of the allotment, the kind you could lie down in and never be found. A forest of achromatic ghost-gums gave her privacy from the top road, lush, subtropical rainforests dappled the hills below and in the far distance beyond lay the blue haze of Moreton Bay.

But it was the view when she tilted her head up that had grabbed her and not let go.

The sky here was like no other sky in the world. Not sky diffused with the glare of city lights, distorted with refraction from tall buildings or blurred by smog. But *sky*. Great, wide, unfathomable sky. By day endless blue, swamped by puffy white clouds, and on the clearest of winter nights the Milky Way had been known to cast a shadow across her yard.

She wrapped her arms about her denim-clad knees, quietly enjoying the soothing coo of butcher birds heralding the setting of the sun.

A mere week earlier her work day would have been kicking off as Venus began her promenade across the dusk sky, masquerading as the evening star. Now that Venus had begun her half-yearly stint as the morning star, Rosie was still getting used to the crazy early starts to the day, and finding it tricky to know what to do with her evenings.

This evening she had no such trouble, filling it ably by reliving her curious encounter with Cameron Kelly. The way one side of his blazer collar had been sticking up as though he'd left the house in a hurry. The way he still hadn't worked out how to stop his fringe from spiking out in all different directions. The way she'd felt his smiles even when he'd been little more than a Cameron-shaped outline. The way her skin had continued to hum long after she'd last heard his deep voice.

She sighed deep and hard, and figured she'd at least get some pleasant dreams out of it!

All of a sudden her bottom vibrated madly. When she realised it was the wretched mobile-phone Adele had made her buy when she'd moved back to Brisbane—lest they live within the same city but never see one another—she picked it up, stared at the shiny screen, and jabbed at half a dozen tiny buttons until it stopped making that infernal 'bzz bzz' noise that made her teeth hurt.

'Rosie Harper,' she sing-songed as she answered.

'Hey, kiddo.' It was Adele. Big surprise.

'Hey, chickadee,' she returned.

'I have someone on the other line who wants to talk to you, so don't go anywhere.'

'Adele,' Rosie said with a frown, before she realised by the muzak assaulting her ear that she was already on hold. 'Girl, I'm gonna throw this damn thing in the creek if you're not—'

'Rosalind,' a deep, male voice said.

Rosie sat up straight. 'Cameron?'

She slapped herself across the forehead as she realised she'd given herself away. If she hadn't been thinking of him in that moment it wouldn't have made a difference. Deep, smooth, rumbling voices like that only came around once in a lifetime.

'Wow, I'm impressed,' he said. 'Did your stars tell you I was going to call?'

'You're thinking of astrology, not astronomy.'

'There's a difference?' he asked.

Her skin did that humming thing which told her that wherever he was he was definitely kidding, definitely smiling.

'So you *are* an astronomer, then?' he asked.

'That's what my degree says.'

'Hmm. I did consider you might be a ticket-seller, but then when I thought back on how hard you were working to not let me buy a ticket I had to go with my third choice of occupation.'

'What was the second?'

After a pause he said, 'Well, it wasn't a choice so much as a pipe-dream. And I'm not sure we know one another well enough for me to give any more away than that.'

The humming of her skin went into overdrive, a kind of fierce, undisciplined overdrive that she wasn't entirely sure how to rein in. She went with a thigh pinch, which worked well enough.

'What's up, Cameron?'

'I just wanted to let you know how much I enjoyed my morning.'

She turned side-on so that her back could slump against the doorframe, and lifted her boot-clad feet to the step. 'So, you did stay for the show. Good for you.'

'Ah, no. I did not.'

Her brow furrowed. Then it dawned: he was calling to say he'd enjoyed the part of the morning he'd spent with *her*. Okay. So this was unanticipated.

When she said nothing, Cameron added, 'I couldn't do it. The wormholes, remember?'

She laughed, loosening her grip on her phone a little. 'Right. I'd forgotten about the wormholes.'

'I, obviously, have not.'

'If one was smart, one might have thought this morning might have been a prime opportunity to overcome such a fear, since you were already there and all.'

'One might. But I've not often been all that good at doing what I *ought* to do.'

First calloused hands, now rebellion. Where was the nice, well-liked Cameron Kelly she'd known, and what had this guy done with him?

'You were in Meg's year at St Grellans,' Cameron said. Meaning he'd been asking around about her.

Rosie unpeeled her fingers from the step and lifted them to cradle the phone closer to her ear. 'That I was.'

'And since then?'

'Uni. Backpacking. Mortgage. Too much TV.' After a pause her curiosity got the better of her. 'You?'

'Much the same.'

'Ha!' she barked before she could hold it back. She could

hardly picture Cameron Kelly splayed out on a second-hand double bed watching *Gilligan's Island* reruns on a twelve-inch TV at two in the afternoon.

'No kids?' he added. 'No man friend to give you foot rubs at the end of a long day telling fortunes?'

Rosie didn't even consider scoffing at his jibe. She was too busy trying to ignore the image of him splayed across her bed.

'No kids. No man. Worse, no foot rubs,' she said.

'I find that hard to believe.'

'Try harder.'

He laughed. Her cheek twitched into a smile. She slid lower on the step, and told herself she couldn't get closer to being physically grounded unless she lay on the dirt.

'You're in a profession which must be teeming with men. How is it you haven't succumbed to sweet nothings whispered in the dark by some guy with a clipboard and a brain the size of the Outback?'

'I'm not that attracted to clipboards,' she admitted.

'Mmm. It can't help that your colleagues all have *Star Trek* emblems secreted about their persons.'

'Oh, ho! Hang on a second. I might be allowed to diss my fellow physicists, but that doesn't mean you can.'

'Is that what I just did?'

'Yes! You just intimated all astronomers are geeks.'

'Aren't they?' he said without even a pause.

She sat up straight and held a hand to her heart to find it beating harder than normal, harder than it had even when she'd been a green teenager. It had more than a little to do with the unflinching, alpha-male thing he'd found within himself in the intervening years. It spoke straight to the stubborn indepen-dence she'd unearthed inside herself.

'You realise you are also insinuating that I am a geek?' she said.

This time there was a pause. But then he came back with, 'Yes. You are a geek.'

Her mouth dropped open then slammed back shut. Mostly

because the tone of his voice suggested it didn't seem to be the slightest problem for him that she might be a geek.

'Rosalind,' he said, in a way that made her want to flip her hair, lick her lips and breathe out hard.

'Yes?' she sighed before she could stop herself.

His next pause felt weightier. She cursed herself beneath her breath and gripped the teeny-tiny phone so tight her knuckles hurt.

'I realise it's last minute, but I was wondering if you had plans for dinner.'

Um, yeah, she thought; *cheese on toast*.

He continued, 'Because I haven't eaten, and if you haven't eaten I thought it an entirely sensible idea that we make plans to eat together.'

Oh? Oh! Had Cameron Kelly just asked her out?

CHAPTER THREE

ROSIE looked up at the sky, expecting to see a pink elephant flying past, but all she saw were clouds streaked shades of brilliant orange by the dying sunlight.

To get the blood flowing back to all the places it needed to flow, not just the unhelpful areas where it had suddenly pooled, Rosie dragged herself off the step and walked out into the yard, running a hand along the fluffy tops of the hip-high grass stalks.

Dinner with Cameron Kelly. For most girls the answer would be a no brainer. The guy was gorgeous. She couldn't deny she was still attracted to him. And there was the fantasy element of hooking up with her high school crush. One of the invisibles connecting with one of the impossibles.

But Rosie wasn't most girls. She usually dated uncomplicated, footloose, impermanent guys, not men who made it hard for her to think straight. She *liked* thinking straight.

The only time she'd ever broken that rule was with a cardboard cut-out of a gorgeous A-list movie star Adele had nicked from outside a video store for her seventeenth birthday. He was breathtaking, he never talked back. Never stole the remote. Never left the toilet seat up. Never filled any larger part of her life than she let him. Never left...

She wrapped her hand round a feathery tuft of grass and a million tiny spores flew out of her palm and into the air, floating like fireflies in dusk's golden light.

Her mother had been the very definition of other girls. She'd fallen for the wrong man, the man she'd thought would love her for ever, and it had left her with a permanently startled expression, as though her world was one great shock she'd never got over.

After years of thought, study and discovery, a light-bulb moment had shown Rosie that, contrarily, the way to make sure that never happened to her was to *only* date the wrong men— those who for one reason or another had no chance of making a commitment. She could then enjoy the dating part dead-safe in the knowledge that the association would end. And when it did she wouldn't be crushed.

So, back to Cameron Kelly. He was gorgeous. He was charming. But most importantly beneath the surface there was a darkness about him. A hard, fast, cool character that he was adept at keeping all to himself. He was fascinating, but there was no mistaking him for some sweet guy looking for love.

And, of all the men who'd asked her out, she knew exactly what she was up against. Cameron Kelly was the least likely man in the world Rosie would again make the mistake of falling for, making him the ideal man for her, for now.

'I haven't lost you, have I?' he asked.

You can't lose what you never had, she thought, but said, 'I'm still deciding if I'm hungry enough for dinner.'

'It's a meal, on a plate. I was thinking perhaps even cutlery may be involved.' His voice resonated down the phone, until cheese and toast was the last things on her mind. 'We can reminisce about average cafeteria food, bad haircuts and worse teachers.'

'When did you ever have a bad haircut?'

'Who said I was talking about me?'

'Ha! You know what? I don't remember you being this ruthless at school.'

'Have dinner with me and I'll do my very best to remind you just how bad I can be.'

Suddenly her hands began to shake. She wiped them down her jeans, dusting off the tiny fragments of plant residue. Then said, 'Where would we go?'

'Wherever. Fried chicken, a chocolate fountain, steamed mung-beans; whatever you want, it's yours.'

'Steamed *mung beans*?'

She felt him smile, and even without the visual accompaniment it made her stomach tighten. But now that she'd reconciled herself to her attraction to him she let herself enjoy it. It felt…wonderful. A little wild, but she had a handle on it. This was going to be fine.

'I didn't want to be all he-man and impose my carnivorous tastes upon you,' he said. 'For all I know you might well be a vegan, anti-dairy carb hater.'

'So happy to know I give off such a flattering vibe.'

'Your vibe is just fine,' he said, his voice steady and low and, oh, so tempting.

She stopped brushing at her jeans and hooked her thumb tight into the edge of her pocket. 'Imagine me as the least fussy woman you've ever taken to dinner.'

'Then I know the place. It's so informal, it's practically a dive. They make the best quesadillas you'll ever have.'

'Mexican for grilled cheese, right?' *How ironic.*

It was his turn to pause. 'It seems I have failed in my attempt to impress you with my extensive knowledge of international cuisine. Mmm. I'll have to up my game.'

Rosie took a moment to let that one sink in. It left a really nice, warm glow where it landed; her hand clutched the fabric of her old black T-shirt against the spot. 'And I guess dinner would be one way of making up for the astrology jibe.'

'I admit, it was hardly gracious.'

'It was hardly original, either.'

He laughed again, the sound sliding through the phone and down her back like warm honey.

The distant tones of a warning bell rang in the back of her

mind, but she was confident enough of him and of herself to say, 'So, yes. To dinner. Sounds fun.'

He gave her the time, and address of the place that made the exotic grilled-cheese, and they said their goodbyes.

When Rosie hung up the phone she realised her knees were wobbling like mad. She slumped down upon the metal step, hugged her arms around herself and looked up.

The clouds had moved on, the colour of the sky had deepened, and several stars had shown themselves. When she hadn't been paying attention, the world beneath her feet had turned.

The world turned some more until night had well and truly fallen upon Brisbane. The bark and bite of peak-hour traffic had subsided to a low growl, and Rosie pulled her caramel velvet jacket tighter around herself to fend off the night chill as she walked briskly down the city footpath. Late for her date.

A minute later the *maitre d'* at the Red Fox bar and grill pointed the way through the bustling bar crowd towards a table along the far wall.

A dive, Cameron had promised. The place was anything but. It was bright, shiny, cool, filled with men with more product in their hair than she had in her bathroom, and women wearing so much bling around their necks she wasn't sure how they kept upright. While she'd been in so many seedy places in her time she could practically write a guide, Cameron it seemed was still very much a Kelly.

She ruffled her hair, wished she'd washed it or put it up, or had a haircut in the past six months, and excused herself as she nudged a group of hot young things out of her way.

Her hand was still delved deep into her hair when she saw him sitting at the head of a loud, rowdy table peopled by ex St Grellans students.

Kids who'd been given sportscars for their sixteenth birthday while she'd taken on an after school job cleaning dishes at a diner. Kids who'd skipped class to shop but had still magically got into universities she'd worked her butt off to attend. Kids who hadn't given her the time of day when, having been accepted to St Grellans, she'd so hoped she'd finally found a place where she might shine.

Suddenly she couldn't for the life of her remember what it had been about Cameron Kelly that had made her convince herself dinner was a good idea. To put on lip gloss. To walk through a cloud of perfume. To wear her nice underwear.

She took a step backwards and landed upon soft flesh. A woman squealed. She turned to apologise, then glanced back at the table where several pairs of eyes were zeroed in on her chest. She wasn't sure if they were collectively less impressed by her lack of top heaviness or the rainbow-coloured peace symbol splashed across her black T-shirt.

But it wasn't so much their eyes she was concerned about as Cameron's. And she remembered why she'd said yes. He was standing, his eyes locked onto hers with a kind of unambiguous focus that was almost enough to send her hurtling towards him like an object falling from the sky.

But not quite.

He was beautiful. He was irreverent. He made her knees wobble in an entirely pleasant way. But she had no intention of going to a place where she had to perform cartwheels to feel remarkable. No man on the planet was worth that.

She offered him a shrug by way of apology then backed into the crowd.

Cameron's backside hovered several inches off his chair as he watched Rosalind disappear into the crowd.

His chair rocked, screeched, and he had to reach out to catch it lest it crash to the ground. His old schoolmate in the chair next to him raised an eyebrow in question.

Cameron shook his head as he brought the chair back upright, and then made a beeline for the front door.

He hit the pavement, looked right then left, and then saw her.

In amongst the night owls in their barely-there attire, she stood
out like a rare bird, striding down the city street in skinny jeans,
flat shoes, a soft jacket nipped at her waist, a multi-coloured
scarf dangling to her knees, her long, wavy hair swinging
halfway down her back, everything about her loose and
carefree. Unpretentious.

And, just as before, having her within reach he felt as
though for now the weight of the world could be someone
else's problem.

He took off after her at a jog. 'Rosalind!'

When she didn't turn, he grabbed her elbow.

She stopped. Turned. A stubborn gleam lit her eyes before
she glanced pointedly at where he still held her arm. But if he
was the kind of guy who got scared off by a little defiance he
wouldn't be where he was today.

'What's with the hasty exit?'

Her chin tilted skyward. 'Would you believe, I suddenly
realised I wasn't hungry after all?'

'Not even if you donged me on the head and hypnotised me
before saying so.'

She kept backing away. He kept following, the sounds of the
bar fading behind him.

It occurred to him that he didn't usually have to work this
hard to get a woman to eat with him. In fact, he'd never had to
work all that hard to get a woman to do *anything* with him. For
a simple distraction, Rosalind was fast proving to be more difficult than he'd anticipated.

But he was born of stubborn Irish stock; he couldn't leave
well enough alone. The effort of the chase only made her vanilla
scent seem that much more intoxicating, her soft skin that much
more tempting, the need to have her with him tonight that much
more critical.

'Rosalind,' he warned.

'Can't a girl change her mind?' she asked.

'Not without an explanation, she can't.'

The stubborn gleam faltered. She glanced down the block at the façade of the bar and bit her bottom lip.

When her teeth slipped away he found himself staring at the moistened spot, transfixed. And imagined pulling her into his arms and leaning her up against the building wall, and kissing her until the dark clouds hovering on the edge of his mind vanished.

He dragged his gaze to her eyes to discover she was still watching the bar, which was probably a good thing, considering his pupils were likely the size of saucers.

As casually as possible, he let her arm go and took a step back. 'So what gives?'

Her chest rose and fell. 'When you invited me to dinner, I thought you meant just the two of us. If I'd known it was to be a class reunion I might have pretended to be washing my hair.'

He followed her line of sight to find one of the guys chatting to a girl lined up outside the bar, but he knew the cheeky bugger was there to give word back to the group. His world was excessively intimate. Everybody assumed a right to know everybody else's business.

Which is why this girl, this outsider, with her refreshing candour and her easygoing, cool spirit was just what he needed.

When he turned back, Rosalind's arms were crossed across her chest and her hip was cocked. Her patience was running thin.

He reached out and cradled her upper arms; the velvet was freezing cold. On impulse he ran his hands down her arms to warm her up.

And at his touch her eyes finally skittered from the bar and back to him. Mercurial grey. Luminous in the lamplight. And completely unguarded. He saw her restlessness, her disharmony, and the fact that she was searching for an excuse to be with him rather than the other way round.

Arrested, he moved close enough to follow every glint of every thought dancing behind those amazing eyes, yet not so close he found himself caught up in the scent of her until he couldn't think straight. And he did his best to be as forthright in return.

'Rosalind, I invited you to dinner because I knew I'd enjoy a night out with you. I chose this place as it makes the best Mexican on the eastern seaboard. As to that lot in there, I had no idea they'd be here; I haven't seen most of them in years. It would have been far more sensible of me to have avoided them once I realised Meg's best mate Tabitha was there, as she can talk the hind leg off a horse, but another fellow is a union lawyer and, workaholic that I am, I saw my chance to talk business and took it. Scout's honour.'

Her eyes narrowed as she asked, 'When were you ever a scout?'

His laughter came from nowhere, shooting adrenalin through his body, putting every muscle on high alert. No longer much caring about keeping himself at a sensible distance from her pervasive scent, he moved in tight and said, 'It's on my to-do list.'

She watched him a few long, agonising seconds before she gave a little shrug beneath his touch. 'Okay, then.'

Okay, then. He took a few more moments to enjoy her sweet scent, her gentle curves leaning into him, and thought about suggesting they skip dinner after all.

He let out a long, slow breath and disentangled himself from Rosalind Harper's corrupting wares. Self-restraint was an asset. It separated men from monkeys, and Cameron from being anything like his father. He needed to get some food into him and soon.

He slid around beside her, placed a hand in the small of her back and did his best to pay attention to his two feet as much as he was paying attention to the swing of her hips beneath his thumb as he herded her towards the Red Fox's red doors.

'It's cold out,' he said. 'Come wait in the entrance while I get my jacket. Then we'll find somewhere else to eat.'

'After all the time you spent convincing me how great the quesadillas are? Not on your life.'

Well, he'd shot himself in the foot there. All he wanted was her. Alone. Distracting him senseless. Now he was going to be stuck in a place peopled by Dylan and Meg's mates, who knew enough about him to want to catch up, and not enough to know which subjects to avoid. 'There's a joint down the road where you can choose your own lobster before they boil it.'

She shook her head, no.

'You sure?'

Her mouth titled into a sexy half-smile as she said, 'Can't a girl change her mind?'

Somehow Cameron found the words, 'Right. Then we'll head inside, and say polite hellos on the way past as we find a table of our own as far away as it can possibly be. Sound good?'

'Sounds perfect.'

'Though, I must warn you, I fully expect them to throw potato wedges at us. If we're lucky they won't have dipped them in guacamole first.'

She snuck a quick look sideways. 'I like guacamole.'

He liked her perfume. He liked her lips. He liked the feel of her beneath his hand. And most significantly he liked the fact that when he was with her his mind couldn't for the life of it wander.

For that alone he promised her, 'Then guacamole you shall have.'

They reached the front of the queue and the bouncer looked up, saw Cameron then opened the velvet rope without hesitation.

Cameron nudged Rosalind with his shoulder and she skipped ahead of him, glancing back with a half smile.

The bar crowd closed in around them. She ran a quick hand through her hair, fluffing it up, and straightened her shoulders like she was preparing to enter a prize fight.

Before he let himself think better of it he took her hand, and as though it was exactly what she'd been waiting for her fingers wrapped tight around his. It brought her back to his side, where her warm body fit in against him.

Images of lips and backs against walls and hot hands rushed in on him so fast one would think he'd been a monk these last thirty-two years.

'Relax,' Cameron said, so close to Rosie's ear her lobe got

goose bumps. 'They won't bite. Though, just in case, I hope you've had your shots.'

She tried to put some air between them, but the crowd kept jostling her back to his side. 'I don't know if you're trying to be funny, as I don't *know* any of them. I barely even know you.'

Her arm dragged behind her as he came to a halt. She let go of his hand and turned to see why.

He was rooted to the spot among the surging crowd, a half-head taller than everyone else, broader of shoulder, and more likely to make a woman tremble with one look than anyone else she'd ever met.

Talk about being remarkable without any effort whatsoever. Maybe once this unnerving-yet-irresistible night was finally over she would have learnt a thing or two about genuine cool.

He slid his hands into his trouser pockets and asked, 'What would you like to know?'

'The highlights so far will do fine.'

His eyes narrowed. 'The name's Cameron Quinn Kelly. Star sign, Aries. Six-feet-two inches tall, weight unknown. I like test cricket more than many consider natural, and can spend hours in hardware superstores without spending a cent and never consider it time wasted. I buy far too many useless things on eBay, because once I'm committed to an auction I can't stand to lose. I'm slightly reluctant to admit my favourite holiday destination is Las Vegas, and I have no shame in saying I have cried during *Dead Poets Society*.'

Rosie took a deep breath. Was it really possible to like a guy that much more after such a simple snapshot? 'You forgot your favourite colour.'

'Blue.'

She didn't doubt it. At some stage that day he'd lost the vest and tie, and the blue shirt hugging his chest was a perfect match for his eyes. It looked so good on him she was finding it hard to remember what else he'd said.

'Enough?' he asked.

She swallowed hard, then quipped, 'That was more than I know about my mailman, and I give him beer at Christmas.'

He bowed ever so slightly. 'Now, before I let you loose upon *my* friends, maybe I should know more about you too.'

Fighting the urge to cross her arms, she grabbed hold of both lengths of her long scarf as she said, 'Rosalind Merryweather Harper. Star sign, Taurus. I'm about five-eight. Weight, none of your business.'

His eyes dropped, lightly touching her breasts, her hips and her calves, before sliding neatly back to her eyes. Her pause was noted, and his cheek curved into the kind of smile that made a girl think of fresh sheets, low lighting and coffee in the morning.

Unnerving yet irresistible. Yep, that summed him up perfectly.

'Merryweather?' he asked.

She grinned. 'It's rude to interrupt. Now, where was I? I've been to Nevada twice, yet never seen Vegas. With all those lights it has to be one of the more difficult places on earth to see stars. My guilty pleasure is Elvis Presley movies, and I was born with seven toes on each foot.'

Cameron's smile wavered. Twitched. Stumbled. His eyes slid to her shoes.

Until she said, 'Gotcha.'

His eyes took their time meandering up her body before they returned to hers.

'Satisfied?' he asked, his voice deeper than the bass notes thumping through the bar.

'Getting there,' she breathed.

The shift of the crowd threw them together. The slide of his cotton shirt against her velvet jacket acted like a flint shooting sparks between them.

She pressed both hands against his chest. 'I'm almost certain somebody promised me dinner.'

He smiled. 'I'm almost certain you're right.'

Then for a moment, the briefest snap in time, she thought she caught a glimpse of the man behind the dark-blue fortress, and saw strengths, knowledge, experience, and hunger far deeper than she'd even imagined. Her fingers curled into his shirt as once again she felt like she was in some kind of free fall.

She didn't like the feeling one little bit.

She slapped him hard on the chest, twice, then with a thin-lipped smile turned away and slid through the crowd.

And then the St Grellans table loomed before her. She recognised a couple of faces—a school captain, a drama queen, the daughter of an ex–Prime Minister. Bless their hearts.

Rosie felt Cameron slide in behind her. 'Do you think for some of them school really was the time of their lives?'

'Was it the time of yours?'

Rosie scoffed so loudly she practically snorted. 'You reeeally don't remember me from back then, do you?'

His silence was enough of an answer. Then he had to go and ask, 'Do you remember me?'

She thought it best to let her own silence speak for itself on that one.

CHAPTER FOUR

AN HOUR and a half later, with the remains of a shared plate of nachos dripping in sour cream taking the edge off her flash-back-phobia, Rosie felt surprisingly serene.

Cameron was a great date—talkative, funny, attentive. And he didn't flinch when she ordered seconds of the quesadillas. That was during the sporadic moments in which they'd been left alone.

A round of drinks had appeared every half hour on the dot, followed by a rowdy toast from the other side of the restaurant. Just about everyone had come over to pay their respects as though Cameron was some kind of Mafia don. And Tabitha stopped by for a chat every time she went to powder her nose. During those moments Cameron held his beer glass so hard his fingertips were the colour of bruises.

Then, when she had him to herself again, he was a different man. The darkness abated, the clouds cleared and he was entirely present. That was the reason she'd sucked up her pride and entered the dragons' den.

In the end she was so glad she had. If nothing else came of the night, slaying some dragons of her youth had been a major plus. Even so, she half-wished they had gone somewhere else after all so that she could have had a little more time with *that* Cameron Kelly.

'Glad we stayed?' he asked.

A fast song came on and Rosie had to lean in to hear him properly. Cameron took her cue and leaned in himself. He was close enough that she could see the ridges in his teeth, a small scar on the bridge of his nose and a slight shadow of stubble at his throat. Tiny imperfections that should have made him less attractive only made him more so.

She smiled. 'You were right about the quesadillas. If they plonked another plate in front of me there is no way I could send them back.'

'Good. Now, for the real reason I invited you to dinner. When do I get my free horoscope?'

She laughed, and flicked the back of his hand so hard he flinched. With reflexes like a cat, he grabbed her offending hand and held it, ostensibly to keep himself from harm, but when his thumbs began running up and down her palm she wasn't so sure.

She manoeuvred her hand away, then sat back and crossed her arms, crossed her legs and remonstrated with herself to keep her feet firmly on the ground where they belonged.

'Pay attention,' she said. 'Because I'm not going to tell you this again. I am a scientist, not a fortune teller. I study the luminosity, density, temperature and chemical composition of celestial objects. My speciality is Venus, the one planet you can still see in the sky after sunrise, about a hand span at arm's length above the western horizon. I am an authority in the field, and if you're not careful one of these times I might turn missish and decide to get offended.'

Cameron looked deep into her eyes, seemingly deadly serious. 'So, tell me, are we alone in the universe?'

She threw out her arms and laughed until every part of her felt loose. 'Are you kidding me?'

'I'm interested in your expert opinion.'

'Here it is. In all my years searching the stars, I've never knowingly seen anything which I couldn't explain. But I'd feel way sillier ruling out the idea than flat-out believing we're alone. The universe is a great, strange and mysterious place.'

He smacked a fist on the table. 'I knew those UFO stories couldn't all be fakes.'

She picked up her napkin and threw it at him. He caught it before it landed in his food. And they sat there smiling at one another like a pair of goons.

An hour later Tabitha was back, perched on the corner of the table, prattling on and on about Dylan's high-school pranks, and Meg's spate of hopeless boyfriends; Cameron had had enough.

The fabulous distraction that was Rosalind Harper only worked when the life he was trying to forget wasn't being shoved down his throat quite so regularly. More to the point, he'd spent enough time with a table between them and an audience watching over them. He wanted to get her alone.

As though she'd sensed him watching her, Rosalind glanced at him over her left shoulder, frowned, then licked a stray drop of salsa sauce from the edge of her lip.

He tilted his head towards the front door. Her eyes brightened, she nodded, and he wished he'd done so a hell of a lot sooner.

He clapped his hands loud enough to cut through Tabitha's verbosity. 'Tabitha, the lovely Rosalind and I are away.'

Tabitha stood up. 'Oh, right. You sure? I just never get to see you any more. Meg says it's because you're always so busy with work, but—'

'Yep,' he said. 'Quite sure. Our after-dinner plans are set in stone. We have to leave immediately.'

Rosalind, trouper that she was, grinned and nodded through his fibs.

Tabitha backed up with a wave. 'Okay, then. Cam, maybe I'll see you at your dad's party on the weekend if you can drag yourself away from work. Rosalind, it was a pleasure. I'll say hi to Meg for you. Both of you.'

Rosalind gave her a wave back, then when she was gone

slumped her forehead to the table, arms dangling over the edge from the elbows down. Cameron laughed as he caught the attention of a passing waitress and mimed the need for the bill.

'And why didn't we go somewhere else to eat?' she asked from her face-down position.

'The quesadillas.'

She clicked her fingers and lifted her head. 'Right. And you have to admit there was nary a projectile potato-wedge in sight.'

'The place should advertise as much.'

She grinned, her eyes sparkling, that wide, sensual mouth drawing his eyes like a lighthouse on a stormy night. It was on the tip of his tongue to tell her as much when the bill arrived.

Saved by the waiter, Cameron took out his wallet, which was closely followed by Rosalind's. He stilled her hand with his. 'Put that away.'

She slid her hand free and hastened to flick through compartments, searching for cash. 'I've got it covered.'

'Rosalind, stop fidgeting and look at me.'

She did as she was told, but it was obvious she was not at all happy about it. And again he got a glimpse of how stubborn she could be.

'I invited you out tonight, so it's my treat. Let me play the gentleman,' he insisted. 'It's not all that often I get the chance. Please.'

It was the 'please' that got to her. Her flinty-grey eyes turned to soft molten-silver and finally she let go of the death grip on her wallet. 'Fine; that would be lovely. Thanks.'

He threw cash on the table. As she eyed the pile, she brightened. 'But you have to let me look after the tip.'

'Too late; I've already added fifteen percent.'

'Why not twenty?'

'Fifteen's customary.'

'Tips shouldn't be just customary. They can make the difference between the underpaid kitchen staff, out there right now washing our dirty dishes, paying rent this week or not.'

Cameron blinked. Forthright, stubborn, *and* opinionated. He tried to reconcile that with the playful, uninhibited girl he'd thought he'd picked up at the planetarium, and found he could not.

What did it matter? Whatever she was, it was working for him. He said, 'So the tip comes to…?'

'Fourteen-ninety,' Rosalind said a split second before he did. She threw another twenty dollars on the table before he had the chance to try, and glanced at him with a half smile. 'Beat ya.'

'Geek,' he said, low enough only she could hear.

As she put her wallet away she grinned, then leaned in towards him. 'Let's blow this joint before Tabitha comes back.'

'Excellent plan.'

Cameron stuck close as he herded Rosalind back through the crowd, partly to protect her from the flailing arms of dancers and chatters alike, but mostly because being close to her felt so damn good.

'So, what now?' she asked.

He moved closer until he was deep inside her personal space. 'Lady's choice.'

She licked her bottom lip, the move so subtle he almost missed it. 'Okay. But dessert is most definitely on me.'

She turned and practically bounced ahead of him.

The image of her wearing nothing but strategically placed curls of chocolate was distracting in a way he might never get over.

Cameron waved a hand towards a large, red plastic toadstool in the universal courtyard outside the Bacio Bacio gelataria on South Bank.

Rosalind sat upon it, knees pressed together, ankles shoulder-width apart, sucking cinnamon-and-hazelnut fla-voured *gelato* off her upside-down spoon.

He had straight vanilla. He'd been craving it all day.

As the rich taste melted on his tongue, he let out a deep breath through his nose and stared across the river at his city. His eyes roved over the three skyscrapers he'd built, the two others he now owned, and through the gaps which would soon be filled with more incomparable monoliths he had in the planning.

'Some view, don't you think?' he said, his voice rough with pride.

Rosalind squinted up at the sky and frowned.

Cameron said, 'Try ninety-degrees down.'

'Oh.' Her chin tilted and her nose screwed up as she watched the red and white lights of a hundred cars ease quietly across the Riverside Expressway. 'What am I missing?'

He held a hand towards the shimmer of a trillion glass panels covering the irregular array of buildings. 'Only the most stunning view in existence.'

She stared at it a few moments longer as she nonchalantly tapped her spoon against her mouth. 'I see little boxes inside big boxes. No air. No light. No charm.'

Cameron shifted on his spot on the toadstool. 'I am in the business of building the big boxes. Skyscrapers are my game.'

She turned to look at him, resting her chin on her shoulder, a lock of her long, wavy hair swinging gently down her cheek. 'Sorry.'

'Apology accepted.'

'Though…'

'Yes?'

'A city is a finite thing. Some day, in the not too distant future, someone like you will come along and tear down your building to make a bigger one. Doesn't that feel like wasted effort?'

He laughed, right from his gut and out into the soft, dark silence. 'You sure don't pull your punches, do you?'

Her cheek lifted into a smile—a smile that made him want to reach out and entwine his fingers in her kinky tresses.

Before he had the chance, she shook her hair back and looked out at the city. 'Growing up, my only chance at being heard was by having something remarkable to say.'

'I hear that. Big family?'

'Like yours, you mean? Ah, no. My mother and I did not ski

together, or turn on the City Hall Christmas-tree lights together. My mum cleaned houses and waited tables and took in ironing, and I can't remember five times we ate dinner together. Much of the time she had other things on her mind.'

She glanced back at him, the reflection of the river creating silver waves in her eyes. And she smiled. No self-pity; no asking for compassion. Only Rosalind Harper just as she was, wide open.

While he sat there, the most mistrustful man on the planet. The secrets he'd kept had led him to play his cards close to his chest his whole life. Hell, he had three accountants so that no one man knew where he kept all his money.

She hid nothing. Not her thoughts, her past, her flaws, her quirks. He wondered what it might feel like to be that transparent. To leave it up to others to take you or leave you.

Oh, he wanted to take her. Badly. But though a level of shared confidence came with them having gone to the same school, and though he was attracted to her to the point of distraction, and though she made him laugh more than any woman he'd ever met, there was nothing he wanted bad enough to make him quit his discretion.

He tightened all the bits of himself that seemed to loosen around her, as he gave as little and as much as he could. 'Is this where you expect me to try to convince you how difficult my childhood was?'

'Cameron,' she said, white puffs of air shooting from her now down-turned lips. 'I have no expectations of you whatsoever.'

And, just like that, tension pulled tight between them. It was so sudden, so strong, he felt a physical need to lean away, but the invisible thread that had bound them together from the beginning refused to break.

He finally figured out what that thread was.

He'd convinced himself he'd been merrily indulging in an attraction to a pretty girl with a smart mouth. He should have known that wouldn't be enough to tempt him. He was a serious man, and, beneath the loose Botticelli hair, the uncensored wry wit and carefree, sultry clothes, Rosalind Harper's serious streak ran as deep as a river.

It would no doubt make for further unpleasant clashes; it would mean continuously avoiding the trap of deep discussions.

Unless he walked away now.

His shoes pressed into the ground, and his body clenched in preparation for pushing away. Then his eyes found hers. Shards of unclouded moonlight sliced through the round silver irises. She had never looked away, never backed down. Who was this woman?

The wind gentled, softened, and took with it a measure of the tension. It tickled at his hair, sending hers flickering across her face. Before he found a reason not to, he reached out and swept it back behind her ear. Her hair was as soft as he'd imagined, kinky and thick and silken.

Her chest rose, her lips parted, her eyes burned. Seconds ago he was ready to walk away. Now he wanted to kiss her so badly he was sure he could already taste her on his tongue. He let his hand drop away.

Rosalind turned back to face the river. She scooped *gelato* onto her spoon and shoved it into her mouth, as though cooling her own tongue. Then from the corner of her mouth she said, 'Am I alone in thinking that got a little heated for a bit?'

'That it did,' he drawled.

She nodded and let the spoon rattle about in her mouth. 'That wasn't me trying to be particularly remarkable.'

'Mmm. I didn't think so.'

She laughed through her nose. 'Thank goodness, then; neither of us is perfect.'

Cameron had to laugh right along with her. It was the best tension-release there was. The best one could indulge in in public, anyway.

Rosie gripped her spoon with her teeth and said, 'Speaking of not being perfect…'

Cameron gave in, stuffed his napkin into his half-finished tub and tossed it in the bin, the makeshift-sweet bite of vanilla no longer cutting it when he had the real thing right in front of him.

She watched the cup with wide eyes. 'What on earth did you do that for?'

'Because I get the feeling I'll need both hands to defend myself against whatever's coming next.'

She held a hand over her mouth as she laughed to hold in the melted *gelato*.

'Come on,' he said, beckoning her by curling his fingers into his upturned palms. 'Get it off your chest now while I'm still in a state of semi-shock.'

She lifted her bottom to tuck her foot beneath, her body curling and shifting, the fabric of her T-shirt pulling tight across her lean curves. 'Okay. Sharing family stories shouldn't be like flint to dry leaves; it should be in the normal range of conversation on a date.'

He pulled his gaze back up to her face and reminded himself she was no intellectual small-fry. 'I like to think a normal range includes favourite movies, a bit about work and a few *double entendres* to keep it interesting.'

Her wide mouth twitched. 'I get that. But people are more than the movies they've seen. We're all flawed. Frail, even. We make mistakes. We do the best we can under the circumstances we've been given. So why not just put the truth out there? I admit I have no dress sense. My dad was never around. My mum was unfit to be a parent. I can't cook. Your turn.'

He broke eye contact, looked across the river and anchored himself in the integrity of concrete and steel, of precise engineering and beautiful absolutes. Everything else he'd once thought true had turned out to be as real as the monsters under his bed. 'You want my confession?'

'No. Yes. Maybe. It sure as hell might make sitting here with you a lot less intimidating if I knew you actually had something to confess.'

He turned back to her, monsters abating as she took precedence again. 'You find me intimidating?'

She raised an eyebrow. 'No. You're a walk in the park. Now, stop changing the subject. I've had the highlights, now give me the untold story before I start feeling like a total fool for thinking you might be man enough to hack a little cold, hard truth.'

God, she was good. She had his testosterone fighting his reason, and no prizes for guessing which was coming out on top.

He kicked his legs out straight ahead to slide his hands into the pockets of his jeans. The moonlight reflected off the water, making the glass buildings on the other side of the river shimmer and blur, until he couldn't remember what they were meant to signify any more.

All he knew was that when his car swung into the botanical gardens that morning he'd been on a search for the truth. And he'd found her.

Maybe he'd regret it, maybe it was the wrong thing to do, but, with his mind filled with that siren voice calling for him to give himself a break, to admit his flaws, to confess…the words just tumbled out.

'What would you say if I told you that I have spent my day certain that my father is gravely ill, and that I've kept it to myself?'

CHAPTER FIVE

THE second the words came out of his mouth Cameron wished he could shove them back in again. Rosalind was meant to be distracting him from worrying about the bastard, *not* inducing him to tell all.

'That the kind of thing you were after?' he asked.

'I was kind of hoping you might admit to singing in the shower,' she said with a gentle smile. But her voice was husky, warm, affected. It snuck beneath his defences and spoke to places inside him he'd rather she left alone.

'Tell me about your dad,' she said.

He ran a quick hand up the back of his hair and cleared his throat. 'Actually, I'd prefer we talk about something else. You a footy fan?'

'Not so much.'

He clamped his teeth together, betting that his stubborn streak was wider than hers. She leaned forward and sat still until he couldn't help but make eye contact. The beguiling depths told him she'd give him a run for his money.

'Look, Cameron, I don't always have my head in the stars. I do know who you are. I get that it might be difficult to know who you can trust when everybody wants to know your business. But you can trust me. Nothing you say here will go any further. I promise.'

Cameron wondered what had happened to a promise of no

promises. Then realised things had been at full swing since they'd caught up, and he'd yet to make that clear.

'Unless you'd really rather talk about football,' she said, giving his concentration whiplash. 'I can fake it.'

Her eyes caught him again, and they were smiling, encouraging, empathetic, kind. He couldn't talk to his family; he couldn't talk to his friends or workmates. It seemed the one person he'd taken into his life to distract him from his problems might be the only one who could help him confront them instead.

He ran his fingers hard over his eyes. 'He was on TV this morning, talking oil prices, Aussie dollar, housing crisis and the like. He flirted with the anchorwoman, and ate up so much time the weather girl only had time to give the day's temps. Nothing out of the ordinary. And for the first time in my life he seemed…small.'

'Small?'

He glanced sideways, having half-forgotten anyone was there. 'Which now that I've said it out loud seems ridiculous. Look, can we forget it? We don't have to talk footy. We can talk shoes. Glitter nail-polish. Chocolate.'

'I want to talk about this. You know your dad. He didn't seem himself. Worrying about him isn't ridiculous. It's human. And you know what? It kinda suits you.'

'Worry suits me?' he asked.

'Letting yourself be human suits you.' She closed one eye, and held up a hand to frame him. 'Mmm. It mellows all those hard edges quite nicely.'

Cameron rubbed a hand across his jaw as he looked harder at the extraordinary woman at his side. He wondered what on earth he'd done right in a former life to have had her offered up before him this morning of all mornings.

She opened her squinting eye and dropped her hand. Those eyes. Those wide, open eyes. Attraction mixed with concern, and unguarded interest. No wonder he hadn't been able to resist.

She looked down into her melting *gelato*. 'Are your family worried?'

'I'm fairly sure they don't suspect.' If they had, there was no way they wouldn't have all been on the phone to him, telling him to get his butt over there.

Her brow furrowed as she tried to fit that piece into the puzzle. But all she said was, 'And your dad? Have you asked him straight out?'

Cameron breathed deep through his nose. *In for a penny in for a pound...* 'That's a tad difficult, considering we haven't spoken in about fifteen years.'

One edge of her bottom lip began getting an extreme workout by way of her top teeth. His physical reaction made him feel all too human.

Eventually she asked, 'On purpose?'

How the hell did she know that was exactly the right question to ask? That no living soul knew how hard he worked to keep clear of the man in question without letting his family know why?

Slowly, he nodded.

'Then why did I think you worked for him?'

'Brendan does. Dylan does. I never have.' *Never will.*

'But you were planning to, right? Economics degree here, then Harvard Business School?' Her mouth snapped shut and her cheeks pinked. Then her mouth drew up into a half-smile. 'My turn again. I confess I overheard you talking to Callum Tucker about it once in the canteen. Of course, it only stuck with me because he said he was going to become a roadie for a rock band.'

Her smile was infectious. A bubble of laughter lodged in his throat. 'Callum is an orthodontist. And I didn't go to business school. I became a structural engineer. After several years in the field, I moved into property development.'

'Impressive.' She blinked prettily. 'Callum Tucker's an orthodontist.'

The bubble burst, and Cameron's laughter spilled out into

the night. Her half-smile bloomed, full and pink and blushing. And, while her hair still whipped lightly about her face in the wind, it had been some time since he felt the cold.

She asked, 'What is a structural engineer, exactly?'

'I warn you, most people tend to go cross-eyed when I start talking structural systems, lateral forces and the supporting and resistance of various loads.'

'Like I don't get blank faces when I get excited about the chemical composition of celestial objects?'

'Sorry,' he said after a pause. 'Did you say something?'

She lifted a hand and slapped him hard across the arm. 'Not funny.'

'Come on, it was a little bit funny.'

She snuck her foot out from under her and placed it next to the other one on the ground, facing him. 'Why not just stick with the engineering?'

'Ego.'

She shot him a blank stare.

'The more things we Kellys see with our name upon them, the happier we are. It comes from having been born out of abject poverty. Generations ago, mind you.'

'How's that? No freshly churned butter on your crust-free organic toast-fingers every second Sunday?'

Cameron grinned. 'Something like that. Ironically, business school would have saved me half the time it took to become profitable when I went out on my own.'

'Nah,' she said, flapping a hand across her face. 'School can only get you so far. In the end you have to throw yourself at the mercy of the universe and take pride in your own ride.'

Cameron let that idea sink in. He was a meticulous planner, demanding control, assurance and perfection from himself and every employee he had. Then again, as a seventeen-year-old kid, he had broken free of the only world he'd ever known. If he hadn't done so he would not be the self-made man he was today.

He nodded. 'I'm damn proud of my ride.'

'Well, then, good for you.'

Her eyes softened, and her smile made him feel like he'd been covered with a warm blanket.

The need to touch her again was overwhelming. Pushing aside her hair would not be enough. He wanted so badly to sink his hand into the mass, pull her in and kiss her until he could taste cinnamon. So, what the hell was stopping him?

The fact that she knew the worst about him certainly didn't help.

Rosalind broke eye contact to eat another mouthful of melting *gelato* and the moment was gone. And, without her striking grey eyes holding him in place, he remembered: there was something wrong with his father. And worse: after a decade and a half spent keeping his whole family at arm's length because the bastard had given him no choice, he still gave a damn.

He blinked, clearing the red mist from his vision and letting Rosalind fill it instead. At first glance, she seemed a 'just what it says on the tin' kind of person—playful, slightly awkward, with an impertinent streak a mile wide. But those eyes, those changeable, mercurial eyes, kept him wondering. He could have sworn she'd changed the subject back there, knowing it was what he needed.

Then, in the quiet, her hand reached out to his. It took him about half a second to give in and turn her hand until their fingers intertwined.

For the first time since that morning Cameron felt that everything was going to be all right.

He frowned. He'd managed to figure that out on his lonesome time and time again over the years. And at the end of the day, when they parted ways, he'd once again only have himself to count on. To trust.

He gave her hand a brief squeeze before pulling his away and leaning back to rest on the toadstool, cool, nonchalant, like nothing mattered as much as it had seemed to matter moments earlier.

'Cameron—'

'You done?' he asked, gesturing to her melting *gelato*.

She licked the inside of her lips as though relishing every last drop of the delicious treat. But her eyes pierced his as she asked, 'Are you?'

He didn't pretend not to understand her. 'Well and truly. I didn't invite you out tonight for a therapy session.'

'So, why did you invite me again?' she asked, with just the perfect amount of flirtation in her voice to make his fingers spontaneously flex.

'It was obvious you were the kind to appreciate the finer things in life.'

'Quesadillas and *gelato*?'

'God, yes.'

He stood.

She did the same, threw her empty container into the bin, pressed her hands into her lower back, then closed her eyes tight and stretched. 'First, I'm a geek. Now I'm obvious. You sure know how to make a girl feel special.'

'Stick around,' he said, his voice gravelly. 'The night is young.'

She stopped stretching and looked him in the eye. Attraction hovered between them like a soap bubble, beautiful, light and with a limited lifespan. Just the way he liked it.

'I could do with walking some of that off.' Cameron patted his flat stomach. 'You game?' He held out a hand.

She stared at it. Then she wiped her hands on her jeans and, after a moment's hesitation, put her hand in his.

Holding hands made him feel like he was seventeen again. But, then again, the fact that he couldn't remember the last time he'd held a woman's hand unless it was to help her out of his car made it feel far more grown up than all that.

As Rosie strolled beside Cameron down the length of South Bank, they talked movies, politics, religion and work. She made fun of him loving a sport that managed to keep a straight face while giving a man a job title of "silly mid-on", while he utterly refused to admit he believed man had ever really set foot on the moon.

But she couldn't get her mind off the elephant in the room; Cameron and his father must have had some kind of falling out. She'd never heard about it in the press or on the grapevine. Yet he'd confided in her. She was caught between being flattered, and being concerned that what had started out as a fun date had become something more complicated so very quickly.

It would be okay so long as she remembered who she was and perhaps, more importantly, who *he* was. He might have fled the nest but he was still a Kelly. He walked with purpose even if that purpose was simply to walk. He had that golden glow that came with the expectation of privilege, while she knew what it was like to struggle, to trip over her own feet and her own words, and to feel alone even in a room full of people. They were manifestly wrong for one another.

They dawdled along the curving path. Moonlight flickered through the bougainvillea entwined in the open archway above. A group of late-night cyclists shot past and Cameron put an arm around her to move her out of their way. Once they were free and clear he didn't let go.

Against her side he was all bunched muscle and restrained strength. His clean scent wrapped itself around her, and it took everything not to just lean into him and forget everything else.

To reforge the natural boundary between them, she asked, 'So, what is it like being a Kelly?'

'What makes you think there is only one way?'

'I'm not sure. Terrible instincts. Stumbling about in the dark only to find the electricity has been cut off. No, wait—that's how it is to be a Harper.'

His steps slowed until they came to a stop. 'Right. Let's stop talking around the real question, shall we?'

Rosie bounced from one foot to another, wondering what can of worms she'd inadvertently fallen into now. 'And what's that?'

'If you were such a poor unfortunate in your youth, while I

was given every opportunity, how *did* you work out twenty percent faster than I did?'

Her head fell back as she laughed into the night. She bobbed her head in the general direction of the Red Fox, wondering briefly if everyone else had made it home to their nice warm beds. 'Don't beat yourself up. Spending time with that lot, how could you not revert to your teenage IQ?'

His eyes narrowed. 'I'm not entirely sure that was in the slightest bit complimentary to any of us.'

She looked him dead in the eye and said, 'Well, colour me surprised. You're not as slow as you seem.'

His cheek slid into the kind of smile that would melt the icy crust of the moon Europa. No wonder she couldn't stop moving. He was always so switched on, he made her feel like there were ants in her shoes.

'So, how did a smart mouth like you end up in such a dry field as astrophysics?' he asked, lifting his foot to lean it against a log on the edge of the garden beside them.

Rosie clasped her hands together behind her back. 'I used to wish upon every star I saw. When I didn't get a trip to Disneyland for my eighth birthday, I gave up on them.'

'Stars?'

'Wishes. Stars I couldn't let go of quite so easily. So, while you hunkered down in your seat shaking like a little girl at the animated wormholes on your planetarium visit, I paid attention. I learnt about Venus, about how she always appeared alone, separate from all the other planets, and only at the most beautiful times of day, sunset and sunrise. That afternoon, I sat in the kitchen window of our apartment block and there she was— bright, constant and unblinking. A free show, for anyone in the world to see. That was the beginning of a beautiful love affair that has lasted til this day.'

Rosie came back to earth to find Cameron standing very still, his eyes dark, intense, with the kind of absolute focus she was certainly not used to being on the receiving end of. She'd been balancing on her toes. She bounced back to her heels with a thud. It didn't help. Those deep, blue eyes looked just as hot from a lower angle.

She started walking again; no dawdling any more. Assuming he'd follow, she said, 'Did you know Venus is the only planet in the solar system named after a woman?'

'I think I'd heard that.' His voice told her he was close.

'And, with a few exceptions, all surface features take their names from successful women.'

'That I did not know.'

'And that, if you weighed one-hundred kilos on Earth, you would weigh about ninety on Venus?'

'I feel like you're trying to sell me an interplanetary time-share.'

She glanced back and wished she hadn't. When she looked into his eyes she forgot herself. Forgot that their time together was one of the universe's crazier anomalies. And she found herself wishing again. Just for the briefest moment, but each and every time.

He asked, 'So are any other planets allowed a look in, or is this an exclusive relationship?'

She looked up, and the tightness in her chest ebbed away. 'I'm a one-planet woman. Earth and Venus are the most similar in size of the planets in our solar system. They came into being around the same time with nearly the same radius, mass, density and chemical composition. But she has clouds laced with sulphuric acid, a surface hot enough to melt steel, and her surface pressure is equivalent to being a kilometre under the sea.'

'She's one feisty broad.'

'Isn't she?' Having built up a safer distance, she spun to face him, and, walking backwards, said, 'Sorry you asked?'

'Not in the least. So, how long have you been working at the planetarium?'

She fell into step beside him, figuring it best to keep her eyes on the path ahead. 'I don't. I've known the manager there—

Adele, who you met yesterday—since uni, and she lets me camp out in the observatory whenever I like. I travelled a lot after school, and now, being back, having the observatory on hand means I can mix things up.'

'And it's a living?'

She shot him a sideways glance. 'As Australia's pre-eminent Venus specialist, I've given talks at international conferences, guest lectured at universities, and even talked on TV about her. And I've worked freelance for NASA for yonks. So, yeah, I do just fine.'

'You're a humble little thing, aren't you?'

'The humblest.'

He moved alongside her, close enough she could feel the whisper of air from his swinging arm brushing her jacket against hers. Their footsteps found a rhythm; her heart on the other hand felt like it was skittering all over the place. It was a feeling she'd never experienced before, comfortable and sexy all at once. She wondered if he felt that way all the time, if being with him she would too.

Rosie slid her arm out of Cameron's grasp, feigned having to unhook the back of her shoe from her heel, then walked on with a good foot's distance between them.

They hit the end of a row of cafés at the southern end of South Bank, then veered around in a one-eighty-degree arc and headed back towards the Victoria Street Bridge. Towards their cars.

Towards the end of the night.

And Rosie's relief and disappointment at the thought of their date coming to an end ran pretty much neck and neck.

On the other hand, Cameron was feeling strangely content. He would have expected by now to be over the elation that came with revelation, and to have moved on to disappointment with himself for giving into a moment's weakness.

But instead his mind was completely filled with the fact that he was out on a stunning winter's night with a beautiful woman. And, having given up so much of himself, he found himself wanting more from her. To restore the balance? That was the reason he was most comfortable admitting to.

He said, 'What's your relationship with your father like?'

She tilted her face towards him; her hair shifted against his shoulder, long, soft, kinky, fabulous. He breathed in deep to stop himself from ravaging her then and there. She really tried his self-control, this one.

'You ask that question like it should have an easy answer.'

'Complicated man?'

She shrugged beneath his arm. 'I wouldn't know. He and my mum met, married, he left, then she had me.'

Cameron's neck tensed. Not in surprise, but in disillusion at the levels to which some men would sink in the grips of their own self-interest. 'That can't have been easy on your mum.'

'Not for the whole time I knew her. They knew one another less than a year, but she dropped out of uni when she met him and never went back. It was as though she always thought one day he'd come back, and she wanted everything to be the same as when he left.'

'So where did a grown-up daughter fit into that?'

Her smile was as rich as always. Could nothing floor her? 'With difficulty, and tantrums and killer grades. Whatever it took to break through the fog. Mum passed away a few years ago when I was overseas. I wish she was still around so that she could see that I've landed on my own two feet. Him too, actually—which is the nuttiest thing of all.'

Her voice was strong, as though she was telling a story she'd told a thousand times. But Cameron was close enough to feel the tremble beneath the gusto.

'Cousins? Grandparents?'

She shook her head. No blood ties. No fallback. No choice about whether or not to turn her back on the man who'd hurt her...

'But I've known Adele since I was seventeen. She's as bossy as a sister, as cuddly as a grandparent, as protective as a dad ought to be. So as far as family goes, I'm more than covered.'

He held out an arm, an offer, and she sank into him. It took a whole other kind of strength not to lean against her, not to kiss the top of her head.

'Argh!' she said, curling away all too soon. 'The last thing I meant to do was get slushy. You just happened to hit a soft spot.'

She slid round in front of him, out of his embrace, though her hand stayed resting on his arm as though she couldn't break all contact. 'Can I poke at one of yours?'

Okay, so she was touching him because she knew he might try to get away. 'You're asking this time?'

She tilted her head, not to be brushed off. 'You have the kind of family some of us only dream of.'

'You know those suburban news reports when a neighbour says "they always seemed like such a nice family"?'

'I never assumed they were *nice*. They might all be stark raving mad for all I know. Nice seems such a bland word to describe…' She waved a hand at him, her eyes touching on his shoulders, his chest. She blinked quickly as they scooted past the zipper of his jeans.

'Nevertheless there are many members of your family. Talk to them about your dad. Talk to your dad. And soon.'

He jawed clenched so hard his back teeth hurt. 'I have my reasons not to.'

'Which are?'

'Impeccable.'

She stared him down, wanting more, but there was no more he would give.

When on that dark day many years before he'd discovered his father had been cheating on his mother, he'd realised that the man his family held up with such reverence and esteem—the cornerstone of everything they represented, everything they were—didn't really exist. And, even if he wanted to explain any of that to Rosalind, unburdening himself would only hurt the others.

When she realised it would take more than silence for him to talk, she said, 'A few years back my mum accidentally let on that she'd been in contact with my father again. He was living in Brisbane. Had been for years. In all that time, he'd never once bothered to look me up. He passed away before she did, and, ridiculous as I know it is, today I still wish I'd had the chance to meet him—to know him, for him to know me— no matter what kind of man he might have been. I'd really hate for you to one day wake up feeling that way.'

Her big, grey eyes were bright in the lamplight. Dazzling with resolve. Could she really be as staggeringly secure as she seemed?

Either way, this conversation was over. 'I give up,' he said, deadpan. 'You win.'

She rolled her eyes and then bent double from the waist, as if he'd finally exhausted her determination. 'It wasn't meant to be a contest. It was meant to be a cautionary tale!'

'You don't like winning?'

She brought herself back upright and grinned at him. 'Depends on the prize.'

Back on solid ground again, on territory in which he was far more comfortable, it took very little effort for Cameron to think of about a dozen prizes he'd happily provide without breaking a sweat. Or, better yet, sweating up a storm.

'Here we are again,' she said.

Mmm, there they were again.

It took a moment for him to realise she was being literal. They'd reached the end of South Bank, and turning left would take them back to the Red Fox and their cars.

He could do as he'd originally planned, kiss her cheek, thank her for a most enlightening night and get on with his life.

Considering the awkward particulars she now knew about him, and perhaps even more importantly what he knew about her—that she was no more the easy, lighthearted-dalliance type than he was a court jester—that would be the smart thing to do.

But it seemed tonight he'd left his smarts behind at the office.

'Thirsty?' His heart thundered harder than he could have anticipated as he awaited her answer.

'What did you have in mind?' she asked, the matching huskiness in her voice making him feel an inch taller.

'The casino's only two blocks away.'

She looked up at him, all luminous eyes, wide lips, sparkle and street smarts, pluck and temptation. He wondered, and not for the first time, how he'd managed to get through high school without noticing her. He'd been seventeen. Maybe that was enough.

Her nose creased; she nibbled at the inside of her bottom lip and picked at a fingernail, and took her sweet time deciding. He had the feeling she might be smart enough for the both of them.

'So, what do you say to one more stop?' he asked, promising himself it would be the last time.

But then her wide, open eyes gave him his answer even before she said, 'There's a tiny corner lounge on the second floor of the casino where they make hot chocolate to die for.'

CHAPTER SIX

ROSIE'S body clock told her it was some time after midnight by the time Cameron walked her from the beautiful old Treasury Casino to her car. Which meant that barring a cat nap in the afternoon, she'd been up for around twenty hours.

No wonder she'd been delirious enough to agree to hot chocolate. Okay, so if he'd suggested they walk the city til they found a greasy kebab van she would have said yes.

She unlocked her old runabout before Cameron reached down to open the driver's side door.

She threw her bag over to the passenger seat and turned to find him standing close, still holding her door, trapping her in the circle of his arms. Close enough so the street lights above created a glow around his dark hair and kept his face in shadow. But the determined gleam in his eyes could not be hidden by a mere lack of direct illumination.

'Tonight was…fun,' he said.

'Which part? The stream of your friends interrupting dinner. Me annoying you so much you had to throw out half your gelato. Or the bit where I tripped on the stairs at the casino and almost broke your toe?'

One dark eyebrow raised. 'I saw the look on your face when you had that first sip of hot chocolate. You were having x-rated fun.'

'Fine,' she said. 'The hot chocolate was heavenly. For that I will be forever in your debt.'

That was the moment she should have waved goodbye, ducked into the car and hooned home. But, even though she felt her life complicating with every new glimmer of light that fractured the darkness within him, she couldn't will herself to leave.

Heck, after she'd let slip that both she and her mum had worked behind the scenes in restaurants, he'd surreptitiously left a crazy-monster tip for the guy who'd served them their hot chocolate when he'd thought she wasn't looking. How was any girl supposed to just walk away from a guy like that?

Wrong. How could Rosie *not* walk away?

While her will played games, her body came to the rescue as she was forced to reach up and stifle a yawn. 'I'm so sorry. I have no idea where that came from.'

'It's after two in the morning, that's where.'

'It can't be!'

He took her wrist, and turned it until the soft part underneath was facing upwards. A small frown appeared between his brows. 'You don't wear a watch.'

She shrugged. 'Even when I used to wear one it never occurred to me to look at my wrist. So I gave up.'

His gaze travelled up her arm to her face. 'I must look at my watch a thousand times a day.'

'Think what you could have done with your lost time if you hadn't been so centred on knowing what the time was.'

Even in the darkness she could sense the sexy grooves dinting his cheeks as he smiled at her. 'You have a strange way of looking at the world, Miss Harper.'

'I look at it exactly the same way you do, Mr Kelly. Just from a few inches closer to the ground.'

'Perhaps. Though what happens to that information when it gets beyond those gorgeous eyes of yours and hits that wild, wily brain, I'm sure I'll never know.'

Rosie hadn't heard all that much past 'gorgeous eyes'.

Dangerously familiar and long-since buried parts of her began to unfurl, warm and throb.

When Cameron ran a careless thumb over the raised tendons of her inner wrist, he created even more havoc within her. If he thought her mind a wild and wily place, it had nothing on the state of her stomach.

'Rosalind,' he rumbled. Boy, the guy had a way of saying her name…

'Yes, Cameron?' she sighed.

He closed his hand about her wrist and tugged her away from the protection of the car door. The sigh became a moan, thankfully quiet enough that he would have had to be two feet closer to have heard. Two feet closer would mean his lips would have been close enough to kiss.

She stared at them a while in silent contemplation. A good while. So long a while that the night stretched between them like a tight rubber-band, and if somebody didn't speak soon Rosie was afraid it would snap.

'I'd really like to see you again,' he said.

Snap! Rosie's eyes flew north til they met his. Deep, blue heaven… 'Seriously?'

He laughed. She bit her lip.

Just because he used her full name in such a deferential way, and how more than once she'd caught him looking at her like she was the most fascinating creature on the planet, didn't mean she should go forgetting herself. On the contrary, she never intended on being just who she seemed in someone else's eyes.

He said, 'Do you want a list of reasons why, or would you prefer them in the form of a poem?'

She shook her hair off her face and looked him dead in the eye, tough, cool, impassive. 'Is that the best you can offer? No wonder you had a blank night in your calendar.'

'Who says it was blank?' he rumbled.

Rosie's heart danced. She blamed exhaustion. She knew that taking guidance from one's heart was as sensible as using one's liver for financial-planning advice, having witnessed first-hand what listening to the dancing of your heart could do to a woman. If she needed any further reason to call it a day…

And then he had to go and say, 'What are you doing tomorrow?'

Her heart did the shuffle. She tried to concentrate on her liver instead. But it seemed every organ was on Cameron-alert.

'Tomorrow?' she said. 'I'll be sleeping. Eating. Watching telly. Looking up. The usual. You?'

'Working. Working. And working some more. Though I too will need to fit some eating in at some stage.'

'What a coincidence.'

'Dinner, then?' he insisted. 'This time just the two of us.'

The two of them. Didn't that sound nice? She looked skyward, but couldn't for the life of her see a star above the canopy of cloud and bright city-lights with which to anchor herself.

She took care to get her next words just right. 'How about you check you diary, and down the track, if you have a window, call the planetarium and they'll get a message to me, and I'll get back to you if my window matches up, and we'll see how we go?'

He let her wrist go which gave her a moment of reprieve before he brushed a lock of hair from her cheek, his fingers leaving trails as light as a breeze across her skin.

'I need a diary,' he said, 'Like you need a watch. And it would make things simpler if you'd just give me your home number.'

He brushed a lock from the other cheek, leaving his hands resting on either side of her neck, leaving her feeling extremely exposed. She'd had to work so hard in her youth to be seen, she'd never had the need to develop a poker face. But she needed it now. All she could do was look at the top of his shirt, where a triangle of tanned skin peeked out from the expanse of blue.

'Can't do that,' she said.

'Why not?'

'Don't have one.'

'You don't have a home phone number?'

'Too difficult, considering…'

'Considering?'

She paused then, wondering quite how to put it in such a way that a man who'd likely never felt a need to deny himself pleasure for the sake of reason would understand. In the end she really saw no choice but to say, 'I live in a caravan.'

Instead of flinching at the very thought—oh, it had happened to her before!—Cameron laughed. Uproariously. As though she'd turned into all the comedians in the world combined.

Her eyes flew up to clash with his. 'What's so funny about living in a caravan?'

'Nothing at all,' he said, his voice still rippling with amusement. 'I think if you owned some suburban Queenslander or lived in a flash city-apartment I'd have been disappointed.'

He'd moved closer, his face now lit by the reflections in a shop window behind her. 'So, tomorrow night. Dinner. Just the two of us. I'll call the planetarium with a location.'

'You could do that.' She bit the inside of her lip only to find that, now he was within the required proximity, it was practically swollen with the desire to lock with his. 'Though I do have a mobile phone.'

His voice was low and dry as he said, 'Do you, now?'

'I never remember to take it with me,' she justified. 'And it's so ridiculously small that I lose it four days out of seven, so I rarely bother giving the number out. But it's there. If you'd like it.'

'That'll do just fine.'

She bent into the car and fumbled through her bag for her phone, and the slip of paper on which her number was written, as she didn't for the life of her know what it was. Then realised she was giving him a fine view of her tush, and stood up so straight she hit her head on the doorframe.

Pretending she hadn't, she jauntily threw him her phone. He punched her number into his, and when she looked at him blankly he did the same for hers. It made her feel like she was nineteen again, in a nightclub, half-hoping the cute guy would call, half-hoping he'd leave her be.

She shoved her phone back into her bag so roughly her knuckles scraped on an inner zip. She then looked up and directly into his eyes from barely a foot away. Those relentless blue eyes…

Kiss me, she yearned inside her head.

No, don't kiss me. Yearning led to pining, which led to languishing. And that was not for her.

He leaned in.

God, yes, please kiss me!

His warm breath slid past her ear as he pressed firm lips against her cheek. With an undisciplined sigh her eyelids fluttered shut, and she let herself open up just a little, just enough so that she could truly feel the moment. His touch, his scent, his strength. The way he made her feel feminine and desirable just as she was.

When he pulled away, her whole body swayed with him. Her eyelids darted open to find his eyes focussed on her lips with such intensity it took her breath away.

Her tongue darted out to wet her lips, and his eyes clouded over, so dark, so hot. She had two choices: throw herself at him, or remove herself from a situation which suddenly felt like it was getting out of her control.

She slid deeper inside the cover of the car and swung the door between them.

Coming to as if from a trance, Cameron growled, 'I'll talk to you tomorrow.'

'It is tomorrow.'

The darkness brightened but the heat remained as his eyes shot to hers. 'So it is.'

'And time I got home to my nice warm bed.'

His accompanying smile was so broad she had the perfect view of a pair of sharp incisors.

'And you to yours,' she added.

This time his growl came without words.

She took that as the opportune moment to give a noncommittal wave before diving into the car and buckling up while he closed the door for her. The fact that she remembered which pedal was the accelerator amazed her as she drove into the night.

Her head throbbed, her knuckles stung, and the voice in the back of her head pointed out she'd lived in one spot for a while now, and Peru was nice this time of year…

An hour later, after Rosie had realised she was too wired to get any sleep, she took a shower and got changed from her pyjamas back into jeans, a warm jumper, and her mangy brown boots in preparation for heading out to the edge of the thicket in which she often spent her early mornings with a tent, a sleeping bag and her favourite old telescope.

She put the TV on while she made herself some jam on toast, not sure how she hadn't keeled over from a sugar rush from the amount she'd already eaten the night before.

The name Quinn Kelly barked from her TV, and she spun and leaned her backside against her tiny kitchen bench.

She didn't know the man, but he was about the most famous personality in town. A charismatic man, with a deep Australian drawl overlaid with enough Irish lilt for it to be unforgettable. He was outrageously good-looking even with his seventieth birthday just around the corner. She recognised him the moment he came on screen in what must have been a repeat of that morning's financial-news report.

She looked through the crooked smile and stunning blue eyes for a sign that all was not well. Or, more truthfully, for signs that Cameron had been wrong and his father was fine. But, as though Cameron was sitting beside her pointing out the subtle nuances of pain etched across his father's face buried deep beneath the infamous smile, she knew something wasn't right.

She'd lived through the sudden loss of one parent and the permanent loss of another, and she wouldn't wish either situation on anyone. Especially not on the man who'd asked the barista at the casino to put extra marshmallows in her hot chocolate just because he thought she might like it.

She picked up the remote and jabbed at the off switch. The small screen went black. 'They were marshmallows,' she blurted at her reflection in the small, black screen. 'Get a grip.'

She grabbed her backpack and headed out into the frosty darkness.

That next evening Rosie arrived at the mid-city address Cameron had invited her to, only to find there was nothing there. Just a cold sidewalk with a handful of newly planted trees looking drab and leafless in the winter darkness, and grey plasterboard two storeys high lining the entire block.

She banged the soles of her knee-high boots on the ground to warm them, and wished she'd brought a cardigan to wear over her floaty paisley-purple dress. But obviously she'd lost her mind the second she'd agreed to come.

She looked up and down the block. A group of bright young things in even less clothing than she wore skipped merrily across the road, arms intertwined. Their voices faded, then it was just her once more.

Her and her chatty subconscious.

What if he was stuck at work? What if he was alone somewhere, trapped under something heavy? Or, better yet, what if he was about to prove how beautifully unavailable he was, how ideal a choice for a first date, by standing her up on the second?

Just as she was about to give herself a pat on the back for being immensely gifted at picking the right wrong men after all, a concealed doorway opened up within the wall of grey, revealing a figure silhouetted within the gap. A figure with sexily ruffled hair, broad shoulders and shirt sleeves rolled up over the kind of sculpted forearms that made her think this was a guy who knew how to fix a leaky tap.

Cameron. Even cloaked in darkness there was no doubting it was him.

'I'm late. Again,' she said, her voice gravelly.

He pushed the hole in the wall open wider. 'You're right on time.'

She shook her head and hastened across the path. When she was close enough to see his eyes so blue, like the wild forget-me-nots scattered throughout her wayward back yard, he said, 'You look beautiful.'

'So do you,' she admitted before she even thought to censor herself.

'Why, thank you.'

She tucked her hair behind her ear and looked anywhere but at him. 'Where are we?'

'We're not there yet.'

Cameron shut the hole in the wall and locked it with a huge padlock, then passed her a great, hulking, orange workman's helmet.

'You have to be kidding,' she said.

'Put it on or we go no further.'

'I'll get hat hair.'

He glanced briefly at the waves that for once had been good to her and curled in all the right directions. 'While inside these walls, you're not taking the thing off.'

'Jeez, you're demanding. You could try a little charm.'

'Fine,' he said, putting his own helmet on and only ending up looking sexier still in a strong, manly, muscly, blue-collar kind of way. '*Please*, Rosalind, wear the helmet lest something drop on your head and kill you and I have no choice but to hide your body.'

She grimaced out a smile. But all she said as she lugged the thing atop her head and strapped herself in was, 'You're lucky orange is my colour.'

He stepped in and reached up to twist it into a more comfortable position, then looked back into her eyes. He said, 'That I am.'

He smiled down at her. She felt herself smiling back, hoping to seem the kind of woman who could get those smiles on demand. It seemed eighteen hours away from him hadn't made her any more mindful. She wondered if it was too late to feign strep-throat or the plague.

She hoisted her handbag higher on her shoulder and gripped tight on the strap. 'Is this going to be some kind of extreme-sport type of dinner? Should I have brought knee pads and insurance?'

'Stick close to me and you'll be fine.'

Said the scorpion to the turtle.

He tucked her hand into his elbow so that their hips knocked and their thighs brushed, and Rosie felt nothing as straightforward as fine as they tramped over tarpaulins, beneath scaffolding and past piles of bricks and steel girders, until they reached a lift concealed behind heavy, silver plastic sheeting.

Rosie said, 'I feel like a heroine in a bad movie with people in the audience yelling "don't go in there!"'

He waved her forward. 'Go in there. Trust me.'

She glanced at him, at the come-hither smile, the dark-blue eyes, the tempting everything-else. Trust him? Right now she was having a hard time trusting herself.

She hopped in the lift, and for the next one and a half minutes did her best not to breathe too deeply the delicious scent of another freshly laundered shirt. Or maybe it was just him. Just clean, yummy Cameron.

She hoped this date would go quickly. Then at least she could say she'd given it a good old try. And know she could still rely completely on her judgement.

As the lift binged, Rosie flinched so hard she pulled a muscle in her side. Cameron moved to her, resting a hand against her back, and she flinched again. Then closed her eyes in the hope he hadn't noticed.

She felt the whisper of his breath against her neck a moment before he murmured by her ear. '*Now* we're here.'

'Where, exactly?'

'CK Square.'

The lift doors swished open, and what she saw had her feet glued to the lift floor. 'Holy majoly,' Rosie breathed out.

They had reached the top floor of the building, or what *would* be the top floor. The structure was in place, but apart from steel beams crisscrossing the air like a gigantic spider-web there was nothing between them and the heavens but velvet-black sky.

Cameron gave her a small shove to the left, and that was when she saw the charming wrought-iron table set for two around which candles burned on every given surface, their flames protected by shimmering glass jars. A cart held a number of plates covered in silver domes, and a bottle of wine chilled in an ice bucket to one side.

It was all so unexpected she felt as though the lift floor had dropped out from under her.

'Cameron,' she said, her voice puny. 'What have you gone and done?'

'I needed to make up for the farce at the Red Fox.'

And, it seemed, for every mediocre date she'd ever endured in her lifelong pursuit of cardboard-cutout companions.

Cameron guided her round neat piles of plasterboard and buckets of paint to the table. Only when his hand slid from her back to pull out her chair did she realise how chilly it was.

She let her handbag slump to the floor and sat, knees glued together, heels madly tapping the concrete floor.

The second he'd finished pouring her a glass of wine, she grabbed it and took a swig. For warmth. He caught her eye and smiled. She downed the rest of the glass.

'So, how was your day?' he asked, and she laughed so suddenly her hand flew to her mouth lest she spit wine all over the beautiful table. 'Did I say something funny?'

She put down the glass, and with her finger pushed it well out of reach. 'Well, yeah. We're currently sitting atop the world, surrounded by what looks to be every candle in Brisbane. And you're actually expecting me to remember how my day was?'

She looked down, picked up a silver spoon and polished it with her thumb. 'Of course, you've probably had dinner here a hundred times, so none of this is in the slightest bit unusual for you.'

She put down the spoon and sat on her hands. He poured himself a glass of wine slowly, then refilled hers just as slowly. Maybe he didn't feel the tension building in the cold air. Maybe she was the only one second guessing why they were here.

As he pushed her glass back towards her, he said, 'I have eaten Chinese takeaway atop a nearly finished building many, many times when the deadline came down to the wire and every second of construction counted. But my only company has been men in work boots. I'm not sure candles would have been appropriate.'

She slid her eyebrows north in her best impression of non-chalance. 'Did you just compare me with sweaty men? I may just swoon.'

Cameron's eyes narrowed, but she caught a glimpse of neat white teeth as a smile slipped through. 'Eat first, then swoon. I'm afraid this will be a shorter meal than last night. The fact we are here at all at this time of night without supervision means that we are breaking enough laws and union rules to get me shut me down.'

Rosie tried to do a happy dance at the "shorter meal" remark, but alas she found mischief even sexier than smooth talk. She clasped her hands together, leaned forward and whispered, 'Seriously?'

He put the bottle down and leaned close enough that she could see candlelight dancing in his eyes. 'Bruce, my project manager, just about quit when I told him what I had in mind.'

'Just about?'

The eyecrinkles deepened and all breath seeped quietly from her lungs.

'Though he looks scary, Bruce is really a big softie. He huffed and puffed and made me promise we'd wear helmets, and then promptly forgot I ever let him know what I was planning.'

She realised then that this would have taken a lot of planning.

Meaning he'd been thinking about dinner, and more importantly about her, for much of the day.

What had happened to the hard, fast, cool character she was
meant to be dating? And why was she so damn stubborn that
she wasn't running scared right now?

He lifted his glass in salute. She took hers in a slightly
unsteady hand and touched it to his. The clink of fine crafts-
manship echoed in the wide, open space.

She said, 'Here's to Bruce.'

Cameron gave a small nod and took a sip, his eyes never
once leaving hers. The urge to laugh had been replaced by the
urge to scream. This was all so unreal, the kind of thing that
happened to other girls. Nice girls. Not pragmatic girls who'd
deliberately ruined every semi-meaningful relationship by
walking away before the other shoe had a chance to drop.

She allowed herself the luxury of screaming on the inside
of her head, and it helped a little.

'Hungry?' Cameron asked.

'Famished,' she said on a whoosh of air. Her eyes drifted to
the silver-domed platters. 'So, who else did you bribe tonight?'

'A friend owns a place at Breakfast Creek Wharf.' He opened
up the first dome to reveal a steaming plate of something
delicious-looking. 'Scored calamari-strips in capsicum salsa,
topped with quarters of lime.'

Rosie flapped her hands at him. 'Gimme, gimme, gimme.'

Cameron did as he was told and she dove in. At the first bite
the taste exploded on her tongue, sour and sweet, fresh, salty
and juicy. Plenty to keep her mouth full so she didn't have to
talk. And didn't have to hear him say anything else to make her
warm to him even more.

Her eyes shifted sideways to the four other domes, a move
he didn't miss.

'Lobster-tail salad with truffle oil,' he said. 'Followed by
apple and rhubarb tart with homemade vanilla and cinnamon
ice cream.'

She warmed a good ten degrees.

A while later, after she swallowed her last mouthful of what had been the most heavenly, delicious apple pie ever created, Rosie let out a great sigh, folded her napkin on the table and looked up to find Cameron sitting back in his chair watching her.

She wiped a quick hand over her mouth, in case she had a glob of melted ice cream on the edge of her lip. But that wasn't it. He was watching her like she'd watched the lobster tail: with relish for what was ahead.

Those blue eyes of his, so like his dad's.

Her heart squeezed for him so suddenly, she held a hand to her chest. But knowing how it felt to have no father at all was one connection she couldn't will away. She wondered what might happen if someone stuck his father and him in a room together and locked the door. It couldn't hurt, but would it help?

Or should she just mind her own business and be glad he was ever so slightly aloof? Aloof was a good thing. Aloof meant there was no chance of any real deep connection being made. Which was fine. Great, even. Perfect.

Cameron's mobile phone rang, and she jumped.

He glanced at it briefly then ignored it.

It rang and rang, and Rosie ran a finger over the last of the melted, cinnamon-flecked ice cream on her plate, licking it off her finger. 'I think that might be your phone making all that racket.'

'It's my brother Brendan,' he said, jaw tight. 'He's the least likely person in the world to call unless he wants something.'

If she'd thought him aloof before, that was nothing compared with the thick, high wall blocking all access to him now. But it didn't help her situation one bit. If there was one thing she didn't like more than feeling emotionally unchecked, it was being made to feel invisible.

'Unless, of course, it's an urgent family matter,' she said, her voice as rigid as his change of behaviour.

His brow furrowed as he glanced at his phone, already a million miles away from her. 'Do you mind?'

'Not in the least.' She stood, snaffled a sugar-sprinkled strawberry from a bowl and took the opportunity to give herself some much-needed breathing space.

CHAPTER SEVEN

ROSIE had no idea how long she sat on a box crate, nothing between her and the edge of the building but fresh air, watching the world below her winding down.

The Brisbane River curved like a silver snake around the city. White boats bobbing on the river surface looked like little glow-bugs; dark patches dotted within the sparkly array marked out gardens and parks. And ragged mountains in the distance barely altered the gentle curve of the horizon.

The world was whisper-quiet, bar the shoosh of the wind. And above? The moon was hidden behind patchy, leopard-print cloud, and delicate, multi-coloured stars beamed intermittently through the gaps.

A wall of warmth washed against her back. She tensed and turned to find Cameron, his face lit by the quiet moonlight. 'Everything okay?'

'Fine,' Cameron said, in such a way that she knew it was not. She knew it was about his dad. The moment heaved between them. She itched to ask, to know, but the truth was for her the less she knew about him the better. That always made it easier when the time came to kiss cheeks and walk away.

'So what do you think of the view?' he asked, sliding a crate next to hers.

She hugged her knees to her chest and wrapped her floaty

dress tight about her. 'Apart from it giving me a case of adult-onset vertigo?'

He laughed. 'Apart from that.'

'The view is…lovely.'

'Just *lovely*? Not magnificent? Not unmatchable? This floor will be rented out for so much money it makes *me* almost blush.'

'It's pretty. But kind of unreal when surrounded by so much concrete and steel. You really want to see something? Stars so bright, so crisp, so shiny and perfect, that you just want to hug yourself to keep all that beauty locked up tight inside of you.'

As her little flight of fancy came to a close she realised he was watching her with that inscrutable intensity that swept her legs out from under her. Lucky thing she was sitting.

'Where, pray tell,' he asked, 'Can a man see such stars?'

'You're mocking me.'

'I am. Only because it makes you blush, which is a view to match even this one.'

She thanked her lucky stars that he was yet to figure out her blushing had nothing to do with his words, and everything to do with his…everything. As his eyes searched hers, she looked back out into the night.

'Around three a.m. is best,' she said. 'At exactly this time of year. Five-hundred metres down the road from where I live, there's a dirt track leading to a plateau where the land drops away on three sides into Samford Valley. If you look to the south-east you can see the city in the distance. But you won't; you'll be looking up. And you'll truly understand why it's called the Milky Way.'

He breathed deep. 'You'll be there tonight?'

'I'm there every night. Though I must admit, I lasted about an hour this morning before I fell asleep.'

His deep, warm voice skittered across her skin as he asked, 'Tired you out, did I?'

'Hardly. I'm just not as gung ho as I used to be.'

She glanced back at him, and regretted it instantly. The guy was like a strong drink: just one taste and the effect on her body, and mind, was debilitating.

He asked, 'And what are you hoping you might find up there in the sky to be out so late at night?'

She nudged her chin against her shoulder. 'I'm not hoping to see anything. I saw what I needed to see long ago.'

His voice was low as he asked, 'What did you see?'

'That my trifling concerns don't matter all that much to anyone but me.'

'Hmm.' Cameron closed one eye and squinted at her with the other. 'I was brought up believing my family was the actual centre of the universe.'

'You do know the geocentric model went by the wayside around the sixteenth century, right? You've really got to see one of Adele's shows at the planetarium.'

Cameron laughed, and Rosie did too. The sounds joined for the briefest of moments before being carried away on the air.

'Until then, take this home with you—the fault is not in our stars, but in ourselves, that we are underlings.'

Cameron waited a beat before saying, 'Where have I heard that before?'

'Eleventh-grade Shakespeare.'

He blinked blankly.

'Now, come on, you can't tell me you never compared some poor, lovestruck and less-rigorously-educated young thing to a summer's day?'

He leaned forward until his face was a relief map of dark and light. She could see the shape of his hard chest as the breeze flapped his shirt against him, and the worry lines that never truly faded even when he smiled.

Thus she was blithely staring into those dreamy blue eyes when he turned to her and said, 'Thou art more lovely and more temperate.'

Several seconds passed in which she said nothing; she just sat there, desperately searching for the humour that ought to have laced his words. Try as she might, she found none. Instead she found herself drowning in his voice, his words, his eyes, in his possibilities.

But that's not why you're seeing him, she told herself slowly, as if approaching an unknown and possibly dangerous animal. *You might be revelling in the invigorating slaying of invisibility demons of your childhood, but he is still the greatest of all impossibilities.*

She uncrossed her arms and grabbed hold of the edge of the crate, let her feet drop back to the concrete floor and dug her toes into her shoes. 'It's getting late.'

Cameron nodded. 'After Brendan rang, my project manager buzzed.'

'Good old Bruce.' The pleasure that skipped through her when he smiled made her wish she'd kept her mouth shut.

'I promised him my whim had been appeased and we were already on terra firma. Unscathed. I got the feeling he was lying in bed awake awaiting that news.'

He held out a hand. She took it. She didn't realise how cold hers was until it was enveloped in the warmth of his. He lifted her easily to her feet, and time folded in on itself as together they walked through the maze of building materials, blowing out each of the candles.

When they reached the table he scooped up her handbag and lifted it onto her shoulder, and then with her hand still snug in his he led her to the lift.

'Shouldn't we take some of that stuff back downstairs?' she asked, giving one last, longing look at the romantic little alcove before, for the sake of every future date, she did her best to forget it had ever existed.

'It'll be taken care of in the morning.'

'There you go again,' she said, shaking her head. 'Thinking yourself at the centre of the universe.'

He lifted his chin. 'You know what? I'm thinking I might hang onto that thought a while longer yet. The pay's good, and the benefits are beyond compare.'

The lift door closed on the concrete and steel, unlit candles and glowing horizon, and Rosie had to admit the guy probably had a point.

They reached the plasterboard wall and Cameron glanced at the top of Rosie's head and held out a hand. It was only then that she even remembered she'd been wearing the orange protective helmet the whole time.

She groaned inwardly. All those longing glances she'd imagined—the moments his eyes had locked on hers, and she'd seen things therein that had made her feel warm all over and scared her silly—she hadn't even noticed his helmet; she'd been so caught up in the rest of him. All the while she must have looked an utter treat.

'If you are hoping to keep it as a souvenir—'

'No, of course not!' She slid it forward, ran ragged fingers across her scalp and tied the length into a hasty knot at her nape, not wanting to know what kind of red marks were shining across her forehead as she spoke.

'Where did you park?' he asked.

She motioned vaguely with her shoulder. 'Down the street.'

He moved in closer. Or had the moon shifted behind a cloud and made everything suddenly seem more intimate? 'Where? I'll walk you there.'

'I'll be fine. These boots might not be steel-capped but I know where to aim them if I get in any trouble.'

The word 'trouble' almost lodged in her throat. Trouble was the look in Cameron's eyes. Trouble was the slip and slide of desire keeping her from backing away as he inched ever closer. Trouble had become her new best friend the moment Cameron Kelly had re-entered her life.

She leapt up on the only thing she could think of that might give her time to find a reasonable, last ditch, way out. 'I've been meaning to ask—what *were* you doing in the planetarium yesterday morning?'

He paused. She took a thankful breath.

'I'm not sure I should say,' he said.

'And why not?'

'Because it's not going to flatter me any.' And it wasn't enough to stop him any longer. He moved in closer.

Rosie lifted a hand to his chest. 'Try me.'

His eyes narrowed. The weight of him pressed upon her hand. His voice was as low as she'd ever heard it as he said, 'I was hiding.'

'No! Yes? Seriously? From whom?'

'My sister Meg. She was there having coffee with a couple of mates, one of them Tabitha.'

Rosie's laughter split the quiet night. 'Tabitha on caffeine? I don't blame you for hiding.'

His eyes slid down her face to settle upon her lips. Her heart shot into her throat. She shut her mouth. But it was no use; every part of her buzzed in expectation of what it would feel like to have his lips on hers.

'Did you know Venus is the hottest planet in our solar system?' Okay, so she was getting desperate.

He paused about three inches from touchdown.

She went on, 'And, while Venus was the Roman goddess of beauty and love, in Greek mythology she was named Aphrodite, and Ishtar for the Babylonians?'

'That I'm sure I knew. I went to a very good school, you know.'

He was so close now; he breathed out, she breathed in, and the sweet taste in her mouth was his.

'Did you ever see that movie—? *Ishtar*? What was the name of that French actress?'

'Rosalind.'

'I don't think so. I wouldn't have forgotten her name if it was the same as—'

'Rosalind,' he growled.

'Yes, Cameron?'

'Shut up so I can kiss you.'

'Yes, Cameron,' she whispered, but it was lost as his lips finally, finally found hers.

She'd heard how some people claimed they saw their lives flashing before their eyes as they were about to pass over. She'd never really believed it could happen until that moment.

Memories of past kisses faded to dust. Every other man she'd ever thought she'd been attracted to melted into a grey, shapeless nothingness, and the blank slate inside her head filled with everything Cameron as emotion upon emotion crashed over her so fast she couldn't keep up.

She tucked a hand along the back of his neck, letting her fingers delve into his soft, springy hair as she pulled him close. His hands bunched into the back of her dress. And together they shifted and turned until every part of them that could touch did.

The kiss deepened, warmed, and took her breath, her sense and her mind until she curved against him like a sapling defenceless against a strong gale.

Helpless, unprotected, lost…

The wind in her ears began to decelerate as the kiss gentled and fell away. It took a few seconds longer before she was able to clamber her way back to the surface, only to find Cameron's smouldering eyes looking deep into hers.

'You busy tomorrow night?' he asked.

She blinked heavily, trying to remember where she was, what day it was, who she was… 'You need some new material.'

'My material is just fine. Are you free?'

She still needed a moment to gather the last few strands of sense that had not been unravelled by his kiss. She'd known it would be amazing, but she hadn't expected anything could be so stunning that it could sap her of every ounce of judgement so that she stood there wide open, wanting more, taking more, any tiny little bit she could get her hands on.

She licked her lips, took a breath, then said, 'I'm busy every night. Busy busy busy, stargazing and the like.'

'Too busy to have dinner with me again?'

'It's certainly possible.'

'I've never known a woman make me work so hard to pin her down for a simple dinner-date.'

He ran a fast hand through his hair, mussing it up, making him look like he'd just tumbled out of bed. The pure, unadulterated sexual energy that careened unimpeded through her brought her out of her trance quick-smart.

She pulled away just enough so that she could feel where she ended and he began. 'The thing is, Cameron, dinner with you has never *been* simple.'

He trailed one hand up her back to unhook her knot of hair, sliding his fingers through it until it fell down her back. Then he twirled a curl around one finger and let it go. Again and again and again.

He said, 'If you like simple, "yes" is a simple word. Only three little letters.'

Heck, if she was looking for simple, the word 'no' only had two letters. So why was it so very hard for her to say? Because cracks the likes of which she'd never experienced before were appearing in her resolve. So far she was coping okay. She was keeping her feet, she was sticking up for herself. What she couldn't be sure of was at what point the damage would be irreparable.

Or perhaps Cameron Kelly was to be the man who would help her prove to herself just how strong she could be, and how the hard work she'd put into herself to make sure she wouldn't make the same mistakes her mum made had truly paid off.

Less than certain of her reasoning, she still said, 'Fine. Yes.'

His forehead unknotted, and she hadn't even realised how tight it had been as he'd awaited her answer. Unless it was evidence of other concerns, which in the midst of her internal toing and froing she had all but forgotten he had.

'Cameron, is…?' She shook her head, searched for the words that would least likely bring the shutters slamming down between them. 'I'd understand if you wanted to make time for your brothers and sister tomorrow night instead, to talk about…things. Or maybe even to go see your dad in person. I know I'm being presumptuous, but with twenty-twenty hind-sight that would be my next move.'

'Being with you tends to keep me more pleasantly occupied.' He said it with the kind of smile he knew could make a girl's knees go weak. But she wasn't falling for it, not when she'd glimpsed what it felt like to really be with him on the other side of the wall. It was enough to keep her pushing.

'So that would be a no to visiting your dad?'

Cameron's cooling smile said it all.

'Did you even talk to Brendan about it?' she pressed.

His eyes narrowed.

She just raised an eyebrow in return. 'You're not going to scare me off the subject. Being an obnoxious teenager prepared me too well for dealing with stubborn men like you.'

A glint lit his eyes, and the corner of his mouth lifted. 'I'm beginning to see that. Fine. He made no mention of my father's health, but he was quite vocal about the fact that if I don't come to the birthday bash this weekend I may as well relinquish my surname for good.'

His hand on her back slid upwards, the shift of fabric made her body melt back against him.

'Them's strong words,' she said, her voice husky.

He pushed the hair he'd been playing with behind her ear. 'Brendan's been around the longest. He's been indoctrinated. He doesn't know any other type of words.'

'Poor Brendan,' she whispered.

'Poor, poor Brendan.'

He leaned in and placed a kiss just below her ear, and she half forgot what they were talking about. And when he moved to nibble on her earlobe itself she forgot the other half.

An age later when he pulled away all she could remember was that they had agreed to a third date. 'So, where to tomorrow? A spaceship? No, a submarine. It better be your basic, run-of-the-mill submarine or I'm out of there.'

'I was thinking of taking you to the first place I ever built.'

She bit back a yawn. 'Fine. But they'd better serve coffee. Three nights out in a row, and I'm afraid I might fade to a shadow.'

'If that's what it'll take.' With that he pulled her close and kissed her again. This time it was slow, soft, tender, mesmerising. He tasted of white wine and strawberries. He made every inch of her feel toasty warm. In that moment the word 'yes' felt like the easiest word in the entire world.

When he pulled away, he did so with discernible regret.

He groaned, spun her on the spot, gave her a small shove in the direction of her car and said, 'Now get, before today becomes tomorrow and we both turn into pumpkins.'

As Rosie walked down the street she felt Cameron's eyes on her the whole way. He obviously hadn't believed her about her ability with her boots. Or maybe he just liked the view.

She added a swagger for good measure.

CHAPTER EIGHT

THE sun was just beginning to rise but Cameron's backside had already been parked atop a dry, paint-spattered stool for an hour as he earned his keep playing diplomat between Bruce, the project manager, and Hamish, the architect. With a month to go before completion, things were tense.

He slid a finger beneath his hard hat to wipe the gathering sweat from his brow, and was hit with the image of Rosalind wearing one the night before.

With those big, grey eyes and her long hair hanging in sexy waves beneath the orange monstrosity, she'd looked adorable. And he was entirely certain she'd had no idea. As a short-term distraction she was proving to be all he could have hoped for.

'Kelly!' Bruce called out, slamming Cameron back to earth with a thud.

'What?' he barked.

'Where the hell have you been for the past five minutes? You sure as hell haven't been on Planet Brisbane.'

Cameron frowned. But Bruce was right. Spending every spare moment with Rosalind was proving to be mighty helpful at distracting him from obsessing about his father. He just didn't need that distraction spilling over into other areas of his life.

Since he'd been thrown out on his own, his business was his everything. It filled his waking hours, and many of his sleeping ones as well. It was his fuel, his drive, his passion. While on the other hand, Rosalind was…

'Earth to Cameron,' Bruce said, shaking his head.

Cameron mentally slapped himself across the back of the head. Enough, already.

'I'm here,' he growled. 'Keep going.'

Bruce leant against a column and crossed his arms. 'I was just telling Hamish here about your little tryst upstairs last night. Candles? Seafood?'

Cameron all but threw the handful of papers in his hands into the air in surrender.

Hamish pulled up a stool so that he was in Cameron's direct eyeline. 'Please tell me the big man's been telling tales out of school. You did not bring some woman here after hours without proper supervision. Not a month out from signing off?'

Cameron stared hard at his mate. Hamish—who had known him since university, therefore knew him only as the ambitious, focussed, blinkered entrepreneur he had become—stared right on back.

'God, Cam,' Hamish drawled. 'You had to be breaking a good dozen laws, not to mention union rules.'

'You think I didn't tell him that?' Bruce asked.

But Hamish wasn't done. In fact there was a distinct glint in his eye as he crossed his arms and leant back on the stool. 'Cam,' he said. 'The last of the honourable men, brought thudding back to earth by a mystery woman. Who the heck is she?'

Cameron closed his eyes and ran his index finger and thumb hard across his forehead. 'She's no-one you know. And this subject is now closed.'

'Fine with me.' Hamish held both hands in the air, then glanced at his paint-splattered watch. 'I have somewhere else to be.'

'We have work to do, McKinnon,' Bruce cried. 'Where else could you possibly have to be?'

'I have a date waiting for me on the exterior-window

cleaning trestle. She should be at about the thirtieth floor by now, so I'll just go grab the champagne and get harnessed up.'

Cameron didn't even bother telling Hamish where to go, he just slid from the stool and walked away.

'Where's he think he's going?' he heard Bruce ask as he reached the lift door.

'If he's trying to cut in on my date,' Hamish said, 'It'll be pistols at dawn.'

There was a pause, then Bruce said, 'I thought you were kidding about the girl,' as the lift doors closed. Cameron was only half-sorry he missed Hamish's response.

He reached the top floor before he knew it. The lift doors opened to a cacophony of noise as glaziers, construction workers and plasterers chatted, banged, drilled, swore and gave the place the kind of raw energy that usually invigorated him.

It meant progress. Honest work, honestly executed by honest men. Sweat of the brow stuff. He was proud of the healed blisters on his own hands for that exact reason.

But as he hit the spot on the roofless penthouse floor, where the night before Rosalind had sat upon a crate, looking out over his city, and with her mix of ruthless candour and subtle beauty had managed to smooth over his perpetual dissatisfaction, the noise faded away.

He leant a foot against the edge of the roof and looked out over the horizon where streaks of cloud were just beginning to herald the rising of the sun.

He held out his hand at arm's length and a span above the horizon; just where she'd said it would be, there it was: Venus. A glowing crescent in the pale-grey sky.

His hand dropped. Somewhere out there, beyond the borders of the noisy, thriving city he loved, she would be sitting somewhere quiet looking at the exact same point in the sky.

And while she was thinking trajectories, gas clouds and expanding universes, he was thinking about her. About seeing her again tonight. It would be their third date in as many nights, which was more time than he'd spent with one woman in as long as he could remember. More time than he ever let himself see Meg or Dylan.

A thread of guilt snuck beneath his unusually unguarded defences. He'd kept those he loved most at the greatest distance so as to save them from being tainted with the hurtful knowledge about his father's weak character he always carried with him. But something Rosalind had said made him wonder: was keeping them at bay hurting them as much?

If he really wanted to see them he knew where they'd be that weekend, all in the one place at the one time, which was usually an impossible feat.

He ran a hand over his mouth. If he went to his father's birthday party, he pretty much knew what would happen. Brendan would swagger, Dylan would win money on a bet he had made somewhere about the date of his return home and Meg would squeal, leap into his arms, then try to set him up with a girlfriend. And his mother would probably cry.

His stomach clenched on his mother's behalf. The clench turned to acid as he thought of how shabbily she'd been treated by the one person who was meant to care for her. The idea of putting on a show at a celebration of that man's years on earth turned to dust in his throat.

He needed to put it out of his mind for good. He checked his watch. Twelve hours to go before he was due to pick Rosalind up at the planetarium. Not soon enough.

'Cam?'

He turned to find Hamish standing in the lift, holding the door open.

'Anything else you want to go over before I do head off?'

Cameron had to think, the usually crisp, clear list in his head squished at the edges, having been pushed aside by other pressing thoughts. 'If there is, I'll call you.'

Hamish nodded and stepped back into the lift, where he held the door open. 'Unless, of course, you need a different kind of advice. I have some moves the likes of which you could not even imagine.'

'I've got it covered,' Cameron said, his voice gruff.

Hamish nodded. 'Good to know.'

Cameron stretched his arms over his head and shook out the looseness that invaded his limbs, and the wooliness that infiltrated his head whenever Rosalind Harper was on his mind.

He did have it covered. He just needed to find some perspective. His business was his life. His family his cross to bear. Rosalind Harper was a delightful but temporary distraction. Tonight he would make sure those boundaries were clearly redefined.

By the time he joined Hamish in the lift, he was clearheaded and ready to act like the head of a multi-million-dollar business.

When after several seconds the lift had yet to move, he realised he'd forgotten to press the button. He reached out and jabbed it so hard his finger hurt.

As the lift doors closed, Hamish said, 'If you're this scrambled, I'm thinking redhead.'

Rosalind's face swam before Cameron's eyes—her wide eyes unguarded, her smile heartfelt, her kiss like heaven on earth.

'Hair like caramel,' he said. 'Skin like cream, legs that go on for ever.'

Hamish swore softly and Cameron grinned.

On the other side of the city, Rosie peeled her eye away from the planetarium's telescope then stared unseeingly at her open laptop.

The cursor blinked hopefully on a blank screen. Her daily notes about Venus's position, colour, opacity, flares, shadows, and any other nuances her dedicated study was meant to bring forth, were lost within the muddy mire of her mind.

She glanced through the gap in the domed ceiling and stared at the distant patch of sky where Venus's crescent had been before streaks of cloud slid across the view. Though, truth be told, she wasn't entirely sure how long she'd been staring at cloud rather then planet.

She leant her hand on the telescope, leant her chin on her hand and stared at a blank spot mid-air about an inch from her nose. Her mind wandered happily back to the top floor of CK Square. Was Cameron there now? What was he doing? Who was he with? What was he wearing? Was he thinking about her at all?

'Mornin' kiddo!'

At Adele's voice, Rosie jumped so high she landed awkwardly and clunked herself on the chin. She rubbed the spot with one palm and asked, 'What time is it?'

Adele perched on the corner of a desk and shrugged. 'Seven-ish.'

Rosie groaned and let her face land against her forearm, where she got a mouthful of red-and-grey-striped wool poncho. She waved a hand in the direction of her laptop and her voice was muffled as she said, 'I've been here since five-ish and have literally achieved nothing.'

A crunching sound brought her head up to find Adele eating a packet of corn chips. Rosie clicked hungry fingers at her friend.

Adele stood. 'Uh-uh. Not while you're within breathing distance of my telescope. I've already had to explain to the board why we needed to have the mirrors cleaned twice last month. A third time and they'll start looking closer.'

Rosie packed up her gear and dragged herself after her friend into the nearby office, where she slumped into an old vinyl chair. She grabbed a handful of chips then hooked her boots over the edge of the chair.

'So,' Adele said, swinging back and forth on her office chair, eyes narrowed. 'How is it that you, Rosalind "stars in her eyes" Harper spent two hours sitting at that thing without making a single note?'

Rosie licked cheese-flavoured salt off her fingers and stared at her friend wondering what, if anything, she should say. Could say. In the end she went with, 'My mind was otherwise occupied.'

It took less than half a second for Adele to join the dots. 'Who's the poor sod?'

She baulked. It wasn't as though she'd kept her dates from her best friend because they felt too precious; she just hadn't found the time. So if that was true why was she hesitating now? She closed her eyes tight and blurted, 'Cameron Kelly.'

When Adele didn't shoot her down with a snappy comeback, Rosie opened one eye.

'Cameron Kelly,' Adele said. '*The* Cameron Kelly who was here the other morning?'

Rosie nodded.

'Well, fair enough too,' Adele said. 'Those thighs, that voice, those eyes; I've been having some nice dreams ever since myself.'

Rosie nibbled at her lower lip and let her legs slide back to the floor. 'The thing is it's kind of gone beyond nice dreams. We've been out the past two nights. And he's picking me up here to take me to dinner again tonight.'

'So why don't you sound as over the moon about that fact as I feel you should?'

'He's just not the kind of guy I usually go for.'

'Um, he's gorgeous and sexy. And you usually go for gorgeous and sexy. Think about the blond who hung around here every morning last summer, making the place smell like sunscreen.'

'Jay was following the waves down the east coast. His job was over at nine in the morning.'

'Right, well, he was gorgeous and sexy. And last winter…?'

Rosie thought back. 'Marcus.'

'Right! The American professor playing job-swap for three months. Super-duper cute in a leather elbow-patch, reading-Emily-Dickinson-to-you-in-bed kind of way. So what makes this one so different?'

Rosie shrugged.

'Is there something wrong with the guy you're not telling

me? Some physical flaw hidden beneath the designer duds? Some personality deviation one would never expect? It's okay; I can take it. I have fantasy guys in reserve.'

'Well…no. Okay, it's like this—he has that inviolable, lone-wolf aura that makes some men always get chosen captain of every team they join, which I really like. He's resilient, self-reliant, and far too focussed on the intricacies of his own life to even think about searching for the girl of his dreams.'

'He sounds just like you.' Adele nodded along. 'Except the liking girls part.'

'In that respect, I guess, yeah. But then in the spirit of full disclosure he's shared with me intimate details of his private life. And he's the kind of man who opens your car door without being asked. I didn't know they even existed any more. Is a nice streak a personality flaw? No, I'm clutching at straws there. Because the way he kisses…'

Rosalind's voice petered away as she became lost in memories of his sultry, liquefying, unnerving, transporting kiss. There had not been one moment of that kiss that could be blandly described as 'nice'.

'Hey!' Adele called out. 'You seem to have drifted off there at the best part.'

'Use your imagination,' Rosie said.

'Oh, I shall.'

Rosie hunched inside her poncho and wondered about Cameron's best parts. Somehow she knew she hadn't even scratched the surface. And that was fine; he could hardly help it if he was naturally fascinating. It was the ferocity with which she found herself longing to know those parts, and to let him get a glimpse of hers, that had her in a twist.

She began nervously flicking at a crack in the end of one short fingernail. 'So, do I see him tonight or quit while I'm ahead?'

'I'm sorry, was Miss Independent looking for my humble opinion?'

Rosie glanced up. 'I ask your opinion all the time.'

'Sure you do, when you want to know which science journals might suit whatever new paper you've whipped up.'

'I'm not that bad.'

'Ah, yeah, y'are. Hon, you're a rock.'

Rosie stared at her friend, who stared right back. She bit the inside of her lip as she said, 'Yeah. I am. I'm just used to looking out for myself, is all.'

Adele reached out with her foot and gave her a nudge on the leg. 'I know, hon. It's cool. Now, do you really want my opinion?'

'I really do.'

'You said this was your third date?'

Rosie nodded.

'Well, then, yeah you're seeing him tonight!'

The friction between Rosie's jiggling knees suddenly had nothing on the warmth invading her cheeks and her palms, and the searing coil deep and low in her belly.

'Adele, the third-date rule is rubbish. Nothing ever happens in life that you don't allow to happen.'

'So you don't want to sleep with him?'

'I didn't say that, I—'

'Then let it happen, for Pete's sake! Jeez. To think if only I'd been at work ten minutes earlier that day it might have been me having this conversation. Actually, no; it wouldn't. I don't believe in the third-date rule either. The second date is fine with me.'

'Adele!'

Adele held up a hand. 'Can I just say one last thing before I zip my lips for good on the matter?'

'Please,' Rosie said.

Adele bit her lip for a moment, just a moment, but just long enough so that Rosie knew she wasn't going to like what she had to say.

'You like the guy, right?'

Rosie nodded, and Adele patted her on the hand.

'Then consider this,' Adele said. '*He* may be an island, but his family is an institution in this town. Unlike your professor or your surf pro, who both came with convenient expiry-dates built in, Cameron Kelly isn't going anywhere.'

Rosie waited for the heat in her belly to cool to room temperature. But for some unknown reason the idea of Cameron being around a while longer than her normal guys didn't scare her silly.

Which of course only scared her out of her mind.

That evening, as they snaked up the steep cliff-face of exclusive, riverside Hamilton in Cameron's MG, Rosie kept doggedly to her side of the car, arms crossed beneath her poncho, knees pointed towards the outer window, feet bouncing against the low-slung floor.

She'd been pacing outside the front door of the planetarium when he'd appeared through the trees, gorgeous in dark low-slung jeans, a black T-shirt under a designer track-top, sleeves pushed up to his elbows, revealing his strong, sculpted forearms that she found so irresistible. His hair was ruffled, his cheeks slightly flushed from the cold. His heavenly blue eyes had been on her. Focussed. Unwavering.

He'd kept an arm about her waist as he'd guided her to his car, then had hastened to put the soft-top up, reminding her how spontaneously nice he was. Then, just before she'd hopped in the car, he'd pulled her close to kiss her hot, hard and adamantly, and she'd remembered how beautifully *not* nice he could be.

Yet all she could think the entire time was that he was gorgeous. It was their third date. And he wasn't going anywhere.

They turned down a street where mature palm trees lined the perfectly manicured footpath and all the houses were hidden behind high fences and brush-box hedges. The MG slowed to a purr as Cameron pulled up in front of a cream rendered-brick wall. A double garage door whirred open and they slunk inside.

Golden sensor-lights flickered on at their arrival, revealing a simple room with polished-wood floors and just enough room for two cars. Or in Cameron's case a car, a mountain bike, a jet ski and three canoes suspended from the far wall.

He took her hand and helped her out of the car.

When he let go she snuck her hand back beneath her poncho and eased round him to give herself space to breathe.

Cameron twirled his keys on the end of a finger as he opened the unassuming doorway to the left and waved her through. 'Welcome to my humble abode.'

On the other side of the door, at the bottom of a tall, curved floating staircase, lay an open-plan room with shiny blonde-wood floors, a far wall made up of floor-to-ceiling windows and a dramatic two-storey canted ceiling. On the right, a raised granite-and-oak kitchen with a six-seater island bench rested beneath a charming skylight the size of a small car. In a living area on the left was a soft, cream leather lounge-suite that would easily seat ten, and a flat-screen TV that must have been six-feet wide. The fireplace in the corner was filled with half-burnt logs and fresh ash. Outside the windows she could see a large, dark-blue, kidney-shaped pool.

Rosie stopped cataloguing and swallowed. 'You built this?'

'It gave me blisters, took a toenail and dislocated a shoulder, so I wouldn't forget. It was the best education for a guy who would one day have labourers in his employ. My empathy when they whinge is genuine, as is my insistence that if I could do it so can they. Come in,' he said as he placed a hand in the middle of her back and encouraged her to get further than one step down.

Her feet moved down the stairs, past the lounge and to the windows as she stared at the view. Beyond the smattering of orange-tiled rooves meandering down the cliff-face below, established greenery bordered the Hamilton curve of the Brisbane River. Half-baked shells of what would one day become multi-million-dollar yachts rode the water surface. In the distance the Storey Bridge spanned the gleaming waterway, and the city glowed in the last breath of dying sunlight while the moon rose like a silver dollar between the towers.

This place was more than just a building; the personality, the warmth, the lovely, lush detail made it more than a house. It felt like a home.

For a girl who took enormous gratification in the fact that the place in which she slept was just that—a place to sleep, with no history, or memory, or attachment, nothing she would fear losing. It was an extraordinary feeling.

Extraordinary and emphatic. Adele was dead right: Cameron Kelly may appear a lone wolf, but he was a man with roots as deep as his city was tall.

'Rosalind?'

'Do you sleep on the couch?' she said overly loudly, to cut him off.

'My bedroom and the study are in the level above. More bedrooms, wet bar; games room below.'

She nodded. 'Your home is really beautiful.'

'Thanks.' His voice rumbled through the wide, open room, but he might as well have whispered them into her ear, the way it affected her.

He was different from the guys she usually dated in more ways than she'd let on to Adele. No surfer's body or professor's poetry had ever brought her to this state of permanent anticipation and awareness of every detail around her, every tactile sensation, every natural beauty. And worse, neither had the dedicated life she'd led alone.

She gave herself a little shake and decided a change of subject was what was needed if she had any chance of finding her feet again.

She turned with a plastered-on smile. 'So where's this telescope you claim to have—still in its box? A figment of your imagination? A falsehood with which to impress the science girl?'

'It's…unpacked. Though honestly it's always been more decorative than functional.'

She stuck a hand on her hip. 'So it's an expensive dust-collector?'

He winced. 'The night I moved in, I looked through the

thing. The trees were upside down. I gave up and watched the cricket match instead.'

'Ever heard of an instruction manual?'

He stared back at her. She let her gaze rove over the glassware in his clear kitchen-cabinets, anywhere but at those hot, blue eyes.

'Some refractors work that way. You just have to remember that in space nothing's upside down or the right way up. Only your thinking makes it so.' She glanced back at him as she said, 'Your problem is the "centre of the universe" thing you have going on.'

'I have the feeling if I keep you around long enough you'll eventually knock that out of me.'

The very idea created a knot deep in her belly. How long was long enough? How long was a piece of string? How long until she relaxed, for Pete's sake?

She tugged on the fingers of one hand until a couple of knuckles gave helpful cracks. 'So where is it? I can give you a quick lesson.'

'It's in my bedroom.'

'Of course it is. Is there any better place from which to spy on your neighbour's trees?'

'There's only one way to find out.'

She tugged her fingers so hard something popped that she wasn't sure ought to have popped. 'I'll take your word for it.'

She stretched out her tense hands, and again didn't quite know where to look—while he stood at the bottom of the stairs clean-shaven, handsome as they came, oozing cool, calm and collectedness. Pure and unadulterated Kelly.

And in that moment Rosie knew she'd been kidding herself; she'd bitten off far more than she could chew.

Cameron was secure in the lifestyle he'd been born to, while it had taken her half a lifetime and a lot of fight to become half as comfortable in her own skin, and she was still very much a work in progress.

If the two of them came together in the kind of collision she felt was on the horizon, he'd not show a dint, while if genetics counted for anything she could well be damaged beyond repair.

When he threw his keys into a misshapen wooden bowl on a chunky hall-table at the bottom of the stairs, the sound made her jump.

She blew out a stream of air, her eyes scooting over the table to find that it was covered in clutter—a baseball cap, a couple of loose computer back-up-stick thingies on brightly coloured lanyards, a camera bag tipped over and empty, a coffee cup with remnants on the rim and a messy pile of opened envelopes in need of throwing out.

The flotsam and jetsam of a real life. And a reminder that Cameron wasn't just a name, or a bank balance, or an alma mater, or an archetype she could shove into some pigeon hole that suited her.

Above all else he was a man. A real man. Possibly the first authentic man she'd ever known.

Warmth curled throughout her insides, loosening all the immobilised places inside her. The feelings that tumbled in its wake came too thick and fast for her to even hope to herd them somewhere safe. She just dug her toes into her shoes and waited for the waves to stop.

Thankfully Cameron was in the kitchen by that stage, with his back to her and his head deep in the fridge, one hand wrapped about the edge of the door, the other wavering near the top shelf, letting out the cold air and not giving a hoot.

'I had a crazy day today,' his muffled voice said. 'One level of chaos after another, starting with some attitude from your friend Bruce. It's made me so hungry I'd eat the fridge if I had a knife sharp enough.'

Rosie was so addled; if he came out of there with a lasagne he'd cooked for her himself, she thought she might just faint.

He ducked his head round the door and his cornflower-blue gaze caught hers. She blinked and stared right back.

He was gorgeous. And this was the all-important third date. But was she willing to yield to everything that concept entailed, even knowing that afterwards he wouldn't be going anywhere?

As though he knew the exact nature of her thoughts, the corners of his mouth lifted lazily, creating the sexiest creases in his cheeks, adorable crinkles around his eyes and such a provocative gleam in those eyes it was as good as an invitation.

Maybe she hadn't bitten off more than she could chew. Maybe she just had to adjust her perspective on who he was and how much of him she could handle. She just had to trust herself that she'd absolutely know the moment to pull out before she'd gone too far. Or maybe, just maybe, he was worth going over the edge for.

'I have no idea what I was hoping I might find in there,' he said. 'There's not a single thing I know what to do with. How does Chinese takeaway sound?'

Rosie let go at the breath she felt like she'd been holding for the past half an hour. 'Sounds perfect.'

CHAPTER NINE

An hour later Rosie sat at the kitchen bench, three of the four white boxes of noodles empty. She abandoned the final unopened box before leaning against the chair back and laying her hand over her stomach.

Beside her, Cameron laughed. 'For a moment there I thought I might have to throw myself in front of the leftovers to save you from yourself.'

'No fear. I know when to quit.'

Cameron's laughter subsided to an easy smile. And Rosie smiled back. The freak-out that had afflicted her early in the evening had faded to a reminder to take care. Once she'd mentally adjusted the limits of what she could handle, she'd begun to relax into Cameron's effortless company.

He'd long since ditched his jacket, and Rosie her poncho and shoes. A CD played softly in the background. A fire crackled in the hearth. And the conversation fell into a natural lull.

Rosie's naked toes curled around the bottom rung of the stool and her eyes blinked slowly. All snug and warm, the past few nights finally threatened to catch up to her.

'You have a little smudge...' Cameron said, his voice low and soothing.

She opened her eyes to find him staring at her mouth, a hand hovering so close to her lips that they began to tingle. Her tongue darted out to swipe at the left corner of her mouth.

He smiled, frowned, then gently wiped a half-centimetre lower. Whatever speck of sauce he found there he proceeded to lick off his finger. And suddenly sleep was the last thing on her mind.

She leant her elbows on the bench and leant her chin on her upturned palms. 'Of all the places in all the world one can be, how is it that a guy like you ended up staying so close to home?'

His eyes narrowed. 'It's not that close.'

The edge in his voice had her shifting to face him. 'St Grellans is five minutes from here,' she shot back. 'And your parents' house is, what, two suburbs over?'

'The fact that I wanted to live in the finest part of town isn't reason enough?'

'Nope. Not for you.'

He picked up his beer and took a slow sip, watching her over the top of the glass. 'How many days ago did we meet up?'

'Two,' she said.

'But this is our third date?'

She nodded. His cheek twitched, and he took another long sip, his eyes never leaving hers as he let that thought sink in. Her leg began to jiggle beneath the bench.

He put down his glass, but kept hold of it as he looked into the amber bubbles. 'I grew up in Ascot. Meg's still at home, though she stays at Tabitha's bachelorette pad in town half the week. Brendan's in Clayfield, close to his daughters' school. Dylan's place is neck-deep in cafés in Morningside. So you're right; we are all a stone's throw from home.'

She crossed her ankles to stop the jiggling and shoved a hand into her hair as she let her upper arm sink against the bench. 'So why didn't you move to the other side of the city when you had the falling out with your dad? Or the other side of the country, for that matter? Or the world. I've done it, several times over. It's too easy.'

He tipped his glass and let it fall back upright before pushing it away and giving her his full focus once more. 'And imagine where you might have ended up had interplanetary travel been on the cards. I hazard a guess that this place wouldn't have seen you for dust.'

Three dates. That was as long as they had really known each other. She thought she had him figured out, but it hadn't occurred to her til that moment that maybe he had her figured out too.

She wrapped her hands about her shoulders, her fingers sliding against the white cotton T-shirt and digging into soft flesh. 'But we're not talking about me.'

His hand slid along the bench to tap her elbow. 'How about we do?'

She shook her head slowly. 'No need. Unlike yours, my life is all figured out. No more analysis necessary.'

He watched her for a few long seconds before sliding his hand beneath her elbow, and turning her on the spot until she was looking out the window at the view of the Brisbane skyline.

His low, rumbling words brushed the hair against her ear as he said, 'That view of that city is what inspired me to do what I do. I can see almost every building I've built from here, and I spend way more time than I ought to admit to sitting by the pool, fantasising about where the next one should go. And that view reminds me that, while I am creating the future of the city, I need to be mindful not to take anything away from the aesthetic created by those who came before me, and hope one day another developer will do the same for me.'

As Cameron's words came to an end, Rosie felt like she was stuck in a kind of suspended animation. Her eyes were locked on the peaks and valleys of the teeming metropolis glittering brightly in the dark distance. And with his deep words echoing in her ears for the first time she saw the profound beauty he saw. In what he did. And in who he was, the true man deep down inside the fortress.

He swung her back round to face him, one eye closed, his divine mouth twisted in chagrin. 'Was that the biggest load of egotistical clap-trap you've ever heard?'

She shook her head slowly, wondering if he had a single clue how at risk she was to his smiles in that moment. 'That wasn't what I was thinking at all.'

'No?'

'I was thinking that, no matter how much you might like people to think that you consider yourself to be the centre of the universe, you really don't. I'm not sure that you ever have.'

He opened both eyes and lost the humble grin. He let his hand slip away from her elbow, ostensibly to grab his drink, but she knew better. Even before he said, 'Whatever gave you that idea?'

'Why skyscrapers? Why not mini-malls or housing estates or parking garages?'

'The bigger the building, the bigger my…income.' He grinned. Gorgeously.

'See, now you might think you can dazzle me with your jokes,' she said, waggling a finger at his nose, 'And your fancy noodles, but I've realised something.'

He leant a forearm along the counter-top and inclined his head towards her. His voice was deep, dark and beguiling as he said, 'Enlighten me.'

'The pragmatic black-sheep, lone wolf, tower of strength, big boss, cool-as-a-cucumber thing you have going on is all an act. You, my friend, are a romantic.'

Well, now, that was the last thing Cameron had ever expected to be called.

Demanding, ruthlessly ambitious, with tunnel-vision. He'd been labelled all of the above at one time or another. But *romantic*?

Rosalind was so mistaken it was laughable. But by the sureness in her wide grey eyes, and the heavy air of attraction curling out from her and enveloping him, he knew laughter was definitely the wrong response.

Needing a moment to find the right way to let her down easily, he slid from his seat, collected the takeaway paraphernalia, slid the chopsticks into the sink and tossed the cartons into the recycling bin.

Then he stood on the other side of the island bench from her and placed his palms on the granite worktop.

'Now, Rosalind, don't you go getting any funny ideas about the man you might think I am. You'll only set yourself up for disappointment.'

Her lips pursed ever so slightly but her eyes remained locked on his. She was swimming against the current, against all evidence that he was as unyielding as he made himself out to be, but she refused to bend.

His voice was a good degree cooler as he said, 'I'm thirty two and single, and there's good reason for it. I don't have a romantic bone in my body.'

She shook her head, refusing to hear him. 'You create things that by their very definition scrape the sky, each one greater and more awe-inspiring than the last. I might look at the stars every night, but you are reaching for them. Just think about it. Let the idea just seep on in under your skin. You'll find I'm right.'

The light in her eyes… He'd never in his life seen anything so bright. And it hit him then that, though she appeared to be as blithe as dust on the wind, though her bluntness made her seem tough, inside she was as soft as they came. Her absent father, and her mother's inability to let go, had wounded her, and she walked through life with a heart prone to bruising, and he had no intention of being responsible for that kind of damage. It would make him no better than his father.

He grabbed a tea towel and wiped his hands clean. He'd been here before. Well, not exactly here, nor quite so soon, but surely near enough that he knew what he had to do.

Looking into those beautiful eyes had been his first mistake. He moved around the bench and took the edge of her chair and spun it to face him.

Giving in to the overwhelming need to touch her, to tuck a silken wave of hair behind her ear, to make her realise that what he was about to do wasn't her fault but his—that he'd been selfish in letting things flow as they had—was his second mistake.

She leaned into his touch, infinitesimally, but enough that her warmth seeped into his fingertips, infused him with her natural heat. Gave him signal upon signal that she wanted him as much as he, for days, had wanted her. Tempted him beyond anything he'd ever felt before.

Feeling like it might be his last chance before he could stop himself, he placed a hand either side of her face and kissed her hard.

Hating the very sight of himself, he closed his eyes tight, which only made every other sense heighten.

She tasted of honey and soy. Beneath his hands she was warm and soft and everything delectable. And beneath everything else she was struggling. He could feel it in her lips as she let in his touch, but nothing more. Nothing deeper.

Earlier she'd claimed she knew when to quit; it seemed neither of them was that astute.

Cameron pulled back, only so that he could kiss her again, more comprehensively, longer, slower. He had no intention of letting up until she kissed him right back.

It didn't take long.

With a sigh that seemed to tremble through her whole body, Rosalind sank back so that the kiss could deepen. And deepen it did, until all he could see behind his eyelids were swirls of red and black, deep, desolate darkness with no end in sight.

She snuck a soft hand behind his neck, lifted herself from her seat and melted against him. The world of sensation inside his mind lit up until he felt as hot and bright as the surface of the sun.

He held her tighter, fisting a hand into the back of her T-shirt, running another over her bottom, the exquisite softness of old denim making his fingers clench, pulling her closer still. His eyes were shut tight, head spinning, and he was kissing her for all he was worth until he couldn't remember ever doing anything else.

As do all good things, it came to an end.

Rosalind pulled away first, her lips slowly sliding away from his, as though it took every effort she could muster. Her head dropped and she rested her forehead against his chest, her hands splayed over his abdomen.

Cameron opened his eyes, the bright, sharp light of reality slamming him back to earth—the reality of what he'd done and what he'd been about to do.

He laid a gentle kiss on her soft hair as his eyes focussed hard on the perfect precision and crisp, true angles of the floating staircase in the distance, looking for his centre as a builder looks to a spirit level.

But all he could think of was lifting her into his arms, carrying her to his bedroom and making love to her all night long. Hell, once there he knew he'd be happy not to come up for air for days.

This woman was giving him a lesson in the lure of temptation, of the lengths a man might go to in order to satiate the want of the one thing his reason and sense and experience and moral centre told him he shouldn't want.

That pull of dangerously destructive desire, a dimension he'd always feared he might be genetically predisposed to possess, was ultimately why he tucked a finger beneath her chin and lifted her head, and waited until her soft dilated eyes were focussed on his.

And in a firm voice he said, 'Might I suggest after tonight we slow things down?'

There, he'd done it, on the back of the kind of kiss that made a guy unable to think sensibly for hours after. That way she'd know it wasn't as merciless as it had sounded.

Her skin paled and went blotchy all at once. She looked at him as though she'd just been slapped. And the shock in her eyes…

His fingers recoiled guiltily into his palm, then uncurled to touch her face. But she'd already disentangled herself to bolt into the lounge, frantically searching for something in her handbag. Whatever it was he could see by the tension in her neck that it wasn't coming to the surface quick enough.

'Rosalind.'

She held out a hand, which as good as told him to shut the hell up.

Ignoring it, he tried reasoning with her, 'Three dates in three days was pure overindulgence on my part. And you can't tell me you're not exhausted. I saw you trying to hide a yawn not ten minutes ago.'

When she lifted her eyes to his, he was fairly sure all she saw was red. She held her mobile phone to her ear and said, 'Which is why I think now is the perfect time to call a cab.'

'Don't be ridiculous. I was always going to take you home.'

'Really? Was it diarised? Kiss Rosie at nine. Dump her at nine-fifteen. Drive her home by ten. In bed by eleven.'

She turned her back, put in the order for the taxi, then threw the phone into her bag.

'Rosalind. Come on. Nobody's dumping anybody. All I'm saying is that we be sensible and look at where we are going here with open eyes.'

She closed her eyes, took a breath and her shoulders relaxed. Somewhat. But that warm, husky voice that he'd become so used to turned as cold as the river at night as she said, 'You want me to be sensible? Well, you obviously haven't been paying close enough attention. If I'd been sensible I would never have agreed to go out with the guy I had a crush on through high school. That is obviously one fantasy best left unfulfilled.'

Cameron's heart slammed hard and fast against his ribs. She'd had a crush on him? And fantasized about him? His voice was deep and dark when he said, 'Come back, sit down and talk to me.'

She waved a frantic hand across her eyes. 'Please. You were right. I'm just overtired. I get it; we've both monopolised one another's time so much these past days. You're busy and I'm busy, and neither of us ever meant for this to be more than it has to this point been. It's fine.'

In the end all she could do was shrug.

If he wanted out for good, this was the moment. He had no doubt she was just waiting for the word—goodbye. It was a simple enough word. Benign, unambiguous, final.

But he couldn't do it. He couldn't be that cool with her.

Unlike every other woman he'd ever dated, she'd never been cool with him. She'd given him nothing but the complete truth, and she deserved the same.

'Rosalind, it's not you.'

'Where the hell's the damn cab?' She paced to the bottom of the stairs. He followed.

'Rosalind, I need you to hear me out.' He knew it was manipulative, but in order for her not to leave feeling hurt and angry he needed her to hear what he had to say, so he said it anyway. 'Please.'

At the 'please', she turned back to him. Her jaw was tight, her eyes wild with emotion. But at least she stopped walking away.

Having to ground himself if he was really going to say this, Cameron parked his backside against a corner of the lounge and looked out across the city view.

'I was in the eleventh grade when I saw my father come out of a city hotel with a woman who wasn't my mother. As I stood on the opposite side of the street, on my way to meet him at his office after school, he kissed her. Right there on the footpath, in front of peak-hour traffic—my father, who the whole city knew by sight. No thought for discretion or propriety or the woman the world thought he'd been blissfully married to for the previous thirty years…or anyone but himself.'

He blinked, dragged his eyes from the city view and looked to her. She stood still as a statue, those grey eyes simply giving him the space to keep going. Deeper. To places he'd never let himself go before.

'My mother… She had to put up with a lot, being married to a man like my father. The long hours, the ego, having to raise his four headstrong children in public. She did so with grace, humility, and love. So the fact that he could show such contempt towards her, to all of us…'

His fingernails bit into his palms as he fought down the same old desire to take a swing at his father the next time he laid eyes on the man.

'Why I am telling you this, what I'd *like* you to take from this,' he said, 'Is that I won't be like him. I'd rather see you walk away now—right at the very moment I can barely think straight for how much I want to continue what we started back there in the kitchen—if that means not hurting you by giving you false hope that I might one day offer you anything more. I can't. Not when I know that even the most solid relationships ultimately fail beneath the weight of secrets and lies.'

He came to an end and needed to breathe deep to press out the sudden tightness in his lungs. His eyes locked onto hers, her strength keeping him amazingly steady.

'Cameron,' she said on a release of breath, 'You expect *far* too much of people.'

'Only what I expect of myself.'

'I was including you too.'

He shifted on his seat. 'You think loyalty and good faith are too much to expect, even after how your father treated you and your mother?'

A muscle in her cheek twitched but her steady gaze didn't falter. 'For some people they are too much.'

He shook his head hard. 'I'm sorry, but I can't accept that.'

'Then that's a real shame.'

Cameron shot to his feet and ran a hard hand across the back of his neck. This wasn't how this had been meant to go. He'd hoped that by being forthright and upfront with her he'd feel justified in slowing things down, like he'd done right by her. Instead she was somehow making him feel like he hadn't done right by himself.

She tugged her poncho over her head, flicking her hair out at the end and running fingers through it until it fell in messy waves over her shoulders.

His response was chemical. His insides tightened and burned with a need to have her lose layers, not put them back on.

The doorbell rang; her taxi. She slipped her feet back into her shoes then looked back at him.

Her eyes said, *ask me to stay*.

But her tilted chin and tense neck said, *let me go*.

He went back to her eyes. Those beautiful, sad, grey eyes, so wide open he felt himself falling in, wanting more than he knew he could give. He pulled himself back from the brink just in time to say, 'I'll call you.'

She nodded, gave a short smile that held none of the mischief and humour he was so used to seeing therein, and jogged up the stairs without looking back.

CHAPTER TEN

ROSIE was exhausted. Which was naturally manifesting itself in a complete inability to sleep.

The minute the clock beside her bed clicked over to a quarter to three, she dragged herself out of bed.

She wouldn't be able to see Venus until about an hour before sunrise, but it had to be better outside than staring at the low ceiling of her caravan, wondering how on earth she'd let herself get to the point where she'd decided she might be able to allow Cameron deeper into her life at the precise moment when *he* had decided he wasn't sure that he wanted her in his.

She ran her hands over her face, then through her hair, tugging at knots in the messy waves, then trudged into the bathroom to splash water on her face. As she wiped it dry, she caught sight of her reflection in the mirror. Eyes dark. Mouth down turned.

She blinked and for a moment saw herself at fifteen, locked in the bathroom of the tiny flat she'd shared with her mum, and this feeling, the same familiar, cutting pain, crawling beneath the surface of her skin. It wasn't the pain of a girl pining for a man in her life. It was the pain of a girl who'd never been bright enough, good enough, devoted enough to fill the subsequent hole in her mother's heart.

How could an invisible girl like that ever hope to be enough to fill anyone else's heart?

Rosie licked her dry lips, then wiped fingers beneath her moist eyes. Time to go. Focussing on the colossal mystery of the universe would render her woes less important. It had to.

Too cold and too miserable to get completely naked, she pulled her clothes on over the top of her flannelette pyjamas—a fluffy wool knee-length cardigan she'd picked up in a thrift shop years before, a thick grey scarf, a lumpy red beanie with two fat, wobbly pom-poms on top, and the jeans she'd worn the day before. She didn't bother with her contacts, leaving her glasses on instead.

The hike to the plateau with her massive backpack was not in the last bit invigorating. It was cold, uncomfortable, and when she hit the spot the night sky was covered in patchy cloud.

She popped up the one-man dome tent which was just tall enough for her to stand up in, threw in all her stuff to keep the dew away and laid a canvas-backed picnic blanket upon the already moist grass. She set up her telescope. And turned on the battery-operated light attached to her notebook.

She sat on the ground cross-legged, waiting for the cloud cover to open up, revealing a sprinkle of stars.

Time marched on and the sky gave her nothing.

No mystery, no majesty, nothing to take her mind off the world at her feet and all the heartache that came with it. She slumped back onto the rug and closed her eyes.

She and Adele had both been wrong. Cameron wasn't really any different from any of the others. They all left her eventually; location had no effect on the matter.

She heard a twig snap, and her eyes flew open.

It could have been a possum. Or there had long since been rumours of a big cat loose in the area. And crazy axe-murderers were a genuine fear for some people for a good reason.

Rosie was on her feet, spare tripod gripped in her hands, eyes narrowed, searching the shadows, when Cameron appeared through the brush, tall, imposing, stunning. It was as though a girl could simply imagine a man like him into existence through sheer wishful thinking.

'What the hell are you doing here?' Rosalind cried, waggling a big black metallic object Cameron's way.

He snuck both hands out of the warm pockets of his jacket and held them in front of him in surrender. 'I tried calling your mobile several times but you didn't answer. So I called Adele.'

'Adele?'

'She gave me her home number when I first rang you at the planetarium. I assumed in case of emergencies.'

Rosalind glowered, but at least she was lowering her weapon at the same time. 'Sounds like her. Though you've got her motives dead wrong.'

'Either way, she told me how to find you in the dead of the night in this crazy middle-of-nowhere place, where anything could happen to you and nobody would ever know.'

He stepped forward, shoes slipping in the soft, muddy earth. By the look in her eyes—behind glasses that made her look smart enough to be an astrophysicist, yet somehow still her usual effortlessly sexy self—she was far from happy to see him.

He didn't blame her. He'd acted just the way Dylan had when they'd been boys, wiping the chess board clean at the first sign the game wasn't going the exact way he'd intended it go.

After she'd gone, he'd lasted about three hours before his furniture had begun mocking him. The stool she'd sat upon when he'd kissed her stuck out from under the bench stubbornly. The beige rug on which her pink shoes had been haphazardly dumped, and the cream couch where her bright poncho had been suggestively draped, had seemed drab and bare. Even the fire had hissed at him, and, whereas for her it had been roaring, for him alone it had crumbled into a sorry pile of ash.

He'd told himself he felt like there were ants crawling under his skin because she was out there feeling upset and it had been his fault. But the truth was his home had felt empty because she wasn't in it. Because he'd expected more of their night together. Before he'd acted like such a lummox, he'd planned on having more time to familiarise himself with her soft skin, to let her sexy hair slide through his fingers. To know those lips as intimately as he could. And the rest.

He needed boundaries, but they also had unfinished business he hoped to take care of—if he could convince her.

'Can you put down the truncheon?' he asked. 'It's making me nervous.'

Rosalind bent at the knees, set the metal object onto a backpack and stood up, her dark-grey eyes on him the whole time. 'You've told me how you got here, not why. And hurry up. I have to get back to work.'

He picked a reason that she couldn't say no to. 'I was watching the sky through my bedroom window when I remembered you telling me that I hadn't seen stars until I saw them from this spot. I thought, what the hell? I'm awake anyway, let's see what the fuss is all about.'

She glared up at him over the top of her glasses. 'So what do you want to see?'

He was looking at it. But he said, 'Show me something spectacular.'

'You've picked a rubbish night.' She dragged her eyes away and looked up into the clear heavens. 'Huh, well, what do you know? Five minutes ago you were all hiding. But in *he* waltzes and there you all are, all bright and shining and cheerful. Capricious brutes, the lot of you!'

She glowered back down at him. 'Well, go on, then. There it all is for your viewing pleasure.'

Cameron looked up into the clear sky, and there it all was, the Milky Way, spread across the sky like someone had scattered a bag of jewels on a swathe of black velvet.

He looked down at her; her nose was tilted skywards, her chin determined, her long, pale neck and wavy hair glowing in the moonlight. He breathed out through his nose. *Spectacular.*

As though she sensed him watching her, she turned her head just enough to make eye contact. She blinked at him, then leaned down towards the eyepiece and found a bearing using the naked eye. She twirled knobs, gently shifted the lever, changed filters, then with both eyes open pressed one eye to the eyepiece and carefully adjusted the focus.

A minute later she stood back and made an excessive amount of room for him to have a look. He took her place, looked through the lens, and the view therein took his breath away.

She'd given him the bright side of the moon. Craters and plateaus in stark white-and-grey relief faded into the creeping shadow of the dark side. So far away, yet it felt so close.

He pulled away, blinked up at the white crescent high in the sky and said, 'I also came here because I don't like leaving a conversation unfinished.'

He felt Rosalind cross her arms beside him. 'Oh, I think we both had ample opportunity to say what we wanted to say.'

'Can I ask…if I hadn't kissed you…?'

She shivered, and this time he knew it wasn't the cold. He wanted to wrap her up in his jacket, but he knew she wasn't near ready for that. Not yet.

'What do you want from me, Cameron?'

'Truth?'

'Always.'

'I didn't like watching you walk away tonight.'

She said nothing. The conversation it seemed would be all up to him.

'I've been having a great time being with you. I get a kick out of your frankness. You must have noticed that I have huge trouble keeping my hands off you. And none of that has changed. All I've ever hoped is that we might continue to enjoy one another's company for as long as it's enjoyable. And not a minute longer.'

He felt her breathe in. Breathe out. 'And who gets to decide when that minute's up?'

'You can, if it needs to be that way.'

'And if I think that minute has already passed?'

'Do you?'

He looked down to find she was no longer staring at the

moon; she was watching him, her eyes wary, calculating, her mind changing back and forth with every passing second.

'I don't want to hurt you,' he said.

Her chin lifted. 'I don't plan on getting hurt.'

She was talking in the present tense. And, though she wasn't smiling at him, neither was she scowling. He'd done enough. Relief poured through him, its intensity rather more than he would have expected.

'Aren't you cold?' she asked.

And he realised he was shivering. She might have been rugged up like she was about to spend a week on Everest but he was still in his jeans, T-shirt and track top.

'I'm absolutely freezing,' he said. Now he'd noticed it, he really noticed it. He rubbed his hands down his arms and stamped his sneaker-clad feet before they turned to ice.

'You have to make the most of your body heat.'

He stopped jumping about like a frog and asked, '*My* body heat?'

'*One's* body heat,' she reworded.

'I was going to say, that was a line I hadn't heard before.'

'Hey, buddy, I have no agenda here. I was out here minding my own business. You came looking for me.'

Still no smile, but the bite was back. Attraction poured through him like it had been simply waiting to split the dam behind which he'd held it in check.

'I did, didn't I?'

She stared at him, the wheels behind her eyes whirring madly. Finally she demanded, 'Get inside the tent, unzip the sleeping bag, and wrap it around you. It's thermal. You'll be toasty in a matter of minutes.'

'Who knew you had such a Florence Nightingale side to you?'

'You're too heavy for me to carry you back to your car if you freeze to death,' she muttered, then gave him a little shove.

From outside the tent Rosie watched as Cameron's head hit the roof as he snuck inside.

He'd come looking for her. In the middle of the night, along unmarked roads and through wet, thorny bushland, he'd come. That was an entirely new experience. Men had left before but none had ever come back. Not one.

She hadn't had any past experiences from which to extrapolate the right course to take. All she'd been able to do was follow her instincts. They'd gently urged her to let him back in. To understand that his dad's betrayal ran deep and that had caused his panic. And that, now that the boat had righted itself, things would be as they were.

She didn't have time to decide if she'd been cool and sophisticated or simply stupid, as right then his elbow slid along the right wall of the tent, making an unhappy squeaking sound against the synthetic fabric. The next loud 'Oomph,' meant she had to go in after him in case he managed to break any equipment worth as much as her caravan.

He turned and saw her there.

Moonlight glowed through the tight mesh, creating glints in his eyes. Though she soon realised the glints would have been there even if they'd been in pitch blackness.

The pom-poms on top of her beanie brushed the ceiling, while he had to bend so as not to stick his head through the top. She glanced up, saw his hair catching and creating static, went to tell him so, but he reached out to her, grabbed a hunk of her cardigan and pulled her to him. Her breath shot from her lungs in a sharp whoosh as her chest thumped against his.

She desperately clambered for her instincts, hoping they might come to her rescue again, but they were as immobilised as she was.

He dropped to his knees and she came with him. They were nose to nose, the intermingling of warm breath making her cheeks hot. Her heart thundered in her ears. She felt light-headed. Little tornados curled about her insides.

And she knew, as well as she knew her own name, that she'd done the right thing. Their minute wasn't up.

He snuck a hand along her neck, his thumb stroking the soft spot just behind her ear. Her whole body responded, opening to him like a flower to the sun. She immediately contracted in fear at exposure of how much she wanted this. Wanted him. Was willing to tell herself whatever she needed to hear to have him.

But then he leaned in and kissed her. Gently. Slowly. And all the last bits of her that hadn't melted finally did so. She sank into him and kissed him back.

Sensation so astronomical overwhelmed her until she could only pick out pieces to focus upon lest she drown in the delectable whole.

The subtle strength of his hand cupped the back of her head. His breath tickled the column of her neck before he rained kisses over every inch of her throat. Her cardigan tie slithered across her back as he undid it.

She came to from far, far away when suddenly it all came to a cruel halt.

She opened her eyes to find him staring at her chest. Her chest wasn't all that impressive without a lot of help.

'What on earth are you wearing?' he asked.

She looked down to find his fingers enclosed over a fat, furry, pig-shaped button on her pink flannelette pyjama-top.

She slapped a hand across her eyes. 'My pyjamas. Oh God, I was cold, I was lazy. I was feeling sorry for myself.'

'Rosalind.' *The way he said her name...*

She let her hand slip away and looked up into his eyes. His deep, dark, bottomless, persuasive blue eyes.

He slipped the first button from its hole, and her breath caught.

And when he kissed her again she felt so frail she believed she might just shatter into a thousand pieces before the night was through.

Hours later, Rosie stroked slow fingers over Cameron's naked chest while his fingers played gently with her hair.

The rising sun washed beams of gold through the opening

of the tent, leaving his beautiful profile in sharp relief, while she was shielded from the beams' touch by his large form.

So it had to be. No matter how much they each struggled against their true natures, he would always be a child of the light, she of the dark.

Perhaps the only moments they could simply still be together were the in-between moments, right at dawn or dusk, when everything seemed softer, gentler, quieter. When nothing, past or future, mattered more than the moment itself.

A great sadness overwhelmed her. Why, she didn't know. After the night she'd had, she should be feeling anything but sad.

She rested her chin on the back of her hands and in the rosy half-light her thoughts spilled unchecked from her lips. 'I've come to the brilliant conclusion that you're the human equivalent of Alpha Centauri.'

He opened his eyes and her sadness slipped away. He turned his head to watch her, a quizzical smile only adding more character to his beautiful face. 'Would it be in my best interests to ask why?'

She grinned from the top of her mussed hair to the tips of her bare toes. 'I'm gonna tell you anyway. Alpha Centauri appears as a single point of light to the naked eye, but is actually a system of three stars.'

'You think I have a split personality?'

She held up a stilling finger. 'I think there's more to you than the face you show the world. You're also bright, eye-catching and seem much closer than you really are.'

'Eye-catching, eh?' He closed one eye. 'And how long were you lying there coming up with all that?'

She shrugged, her upper body sliding deliciously against his. 'Not long.'

'Mmm.' He lifted a heavy hand and trailed it down her naked back, sending goose bumps popping up all over her skin. 'So how far away is my heavenly twin right now?'

'Four-point-three trillion kilometres.'

His laughter lifted her as it echoed through his ribs.

Rosie buried her blushing cheeks in a mound of sleeping bag. 'I'm sorry. I just compared you with spheres of hot gases. And after all the nice things you just did for me. And *to* me. It seems to have opened neural pathways better left closed.'

'I only have myself to blame.'

She lifted her head and rubbed a knuckle across the end of her cold nose. He lifted his head to kiss the spot.

This was bliss. This made it all worth it. Surely...

She looked directly into his disarming eyes as she said, 'All that Alpha Centauri stuff—I just meant that you've turned out to be not quite who I expected you'd be.'

'A man ought to do his best to exceed expectations wherever possible.'

'Maybe a man ought to, though in my experience not all that many bother to try.'

'Your experience?' he rumbled. 'Now, there's a subject I could warm to.'

He waggled his eyebrows, and Rosie felt like she'd blushed enough for one day. Any more and her cheeks might stay that way.

'This is *not* the time for that conversation.' She dragged herself into a sitting position. She slipped her flannelette pyjama-top on, and quickly added the beanie and scarf, suddenly cold now that she was no longer wrapped in Cameron.

His fingers slunk beneath her top and trailed down her back, creating a slip and shift of heat that made her want to give in and stay, talk, confess, believe...

But, like Alpha Centauri, the four-point-three trillion ways he made her feel safe and secure and precious were illusions all. At the end of the day, she was all she had. And that was fine. She could enjoy him in the in-between times. And that would be enough. If she told herself enough times she might even start to believe it.

'Then how about we put it right up front during a Saturday night drink before my dad's birthday party?' he said.

'Before your who and what?' she asked. Her head whipped round to stare at him, to find him leaning on one arm, bare chest rippling with manly gorgeousness that made her sure the canoe, bike and jet ski in his garage weren't the dust collectors his telescope was.

Her mouth watered. She dragged her eyes back to his—like that had ever made anything any easier!

'My father's seventieth,' he said. 'Something you said has been percolating for a while now. And last night, as I cleaned the floors of my house with my hours of pacing, I made up my mind. I'm going.'

'What did I say?'

'That you spent too long wishing you'd had the chance to know your father, no matter what kind of man he might have been. I need to face the man, to ease my mind. And, since you're the one who convinced me as much, I thought you might like to tag along.'

Rosie breathed in and out. In and out. Not eight hours earlier he'd wanted to cool things down. Now he was making plans whereby she would meet his parents. His whole family. She tried to figure out what he was playing at, but all that beautiful, warm skin was making it hard for her to see the bigger picture.

'Saturday? I can't,' she said, searching the end of the sleeping bag with her feet for her jeans and sighing with relief when her toes hit denim.

'It'll be one hell of a party.'

'I'm sure it will.'

The sleeping bag around her bare thighs slid away as Cameron sat up, and it pooled low around his hips. Staring at the bland wall of the tent, she whipped on her cardigan and did the bow up tight.

He leaned in and pushed her hair aside, laying a small, soft kiss on her neck.

She closed her eyes and tried to ignore the warmth washing across her skin, the grip of his gravitational pull tugging her into oblivion. But it felt too good. He felt so good. So difficult, so dangerous, but so very good.

'Cameron…'

'The truth is, I need you there.'

She squeezed her forehead tight, trying to push away how wonderful those three words—*I need you*—felt.

Once upon a time all she'd wanted was to feel needed, wanted, loved. She'd been a good kid, she'd studied hard, and she'd silently hugged her mum whenever she'd found her crying, even when deep down she'd known it would never be enough.

Since she'd been on her own in the big, wide world all she'd needed was fresh air, food, water and basic shelter. She'd never once felt that need to be needed by anybody else.

Yet now those three little words danced behind her eyes, waving streamers and skipping through fertile fields, singing at the top of their lungs. It had been so long since she'd shoved the wish down so deep inside that the moment it came to the surface it was intoxicating.

'I'll think about it.'

'Don't think, just come,' he murmured against her shoulder.

She extricated herself from his wandering hands and slipped out of the tent, happier to be half-naked beneath the open sky than to see how much more he could get her to promise him from just a simple touch.

'So, I'll pick you up at your place around eight,' he called out.

She found her functional white, cotton briefs hanging provocatively over her tripod, and shoved them into a pocket of her telescope bag. 'Oh, for Pete's sake, fine! I'll go. Are you happy now?'

'Now I am happy.'

All her fidgeting stopped. He might have been playing like he was flirting, but the thread of truth lacing its way beneath his words got to her like nothing else.

She glanced back into the tent to find Cameron was lying back with his arms over his head, his biceps cradling his head, watching her.

'It's black tie,' he said with a grin.

Her eyebrows lifted so fast she almost pulled something. 'Are you intimating *that* might be a reason for me to back out?'

His gaze meandered down her crazy get-up. 'Not at all. So far you haven't found it at all difficult to just say no to me when you really wanted to say no.'

'You have no idea,' she muttered.

'What was that?'

She wrapped the tie of her fluffy cardigan ever tighter. 'Cameron, I'll go with you to your father's party because I'm madly proud of you for listening to my words of wisdom. No hidden agenda. Nothing more. As agreed last night.'

He stared at her for a few moments, then nodded. She was mighty glad he believed her, as she wasn't even close to sure that she believed herself.

She shielded her eyes and looked to the sun, which had risen, making it some time after seven in the morning. The faint crescent of Venus had been hovering above the horizon for some time without even getting a look in.

She said, 'Shouldn't you get going? Don't you have minions to boss around at the worksite? Won't Bruce be lost without you?'

'I'm not so worried about Bruce right this second. How about you?'

'Bruce isn't high on my list of priorities either.'

He smiled. A smile so stunningly sexy that Rosie's knees forgot how to work.

'I meant, do you have anywhere else to be,' he said.

She blinked down at him, arms crossed. 'Um, no. I don't. Because this is my place of work.'

Cameron didn't move a muscle. He simply lay naked in her tent, while she realised that from the minute he'd walked into her glade—all gorgeous and conciliatory, talking of how he couldn't keep his hands off her—she hadn't given her work, her time, her warm bed, her breakfast, or anything else usually so important to her, a single thought.

Warning bells began to chime inside her head, telling her to finish getting dressed. To get moving. To just let him keep the damn tent.

'Then what are you doing out there in the cold when it's still so warm in here?' he asked, flapping open the sleeping bag, leaving room for her.

That was all she'd done for him too—left room. And if that meant having a little less room for herself then maybe that was the price a girl had to pay for getting a man who came back for her.

Rosie bit her lip, weighed her options, became trapped in his eyes, then said, 'Oh, what the hell,' as she tore off her beanie and threw it over her shoulder before she dove back into the tent.

'Now, tell me more about this crush you had on me in high school,' he muttered as he stripped her down.

'I *think* it was you I had the crush on. You were the captain of the footy team, right?'

'No, I was not. Now, stop sassing me and tell me about the moment you first laid eyes on me and your teenaged heart went pitter-pat.'

'Cameron Kelly,' she said on a sigh as he went to work, 'You'll have to do much better than that if you think I'm ever going to spill a single detail.'

He did better. Like a lightweight, she spilled.

And, just as she'd hoped, the warning bells were soon drowned out by the symphony of sensations only this man could make her feel.

CHAPTER ELEVEN

Most of that next day and night Rosie slept like a log. Saturday morning she woke late, crinkled, ruffled, and blissfully replenished in every which way.

It was after lunch by the time she stood staring unseeingly at the window of the designer boutique on the top floor of Queens Plaza.

Adele was puffing when she arrived at her side. 'Sorry, sorry. Lipstick disaster. Don't ask.' Puff, puff, puff. 'What's the big emergency?'

'I have to buy a new dress to wear tonight.'

'I know a dress from a pair of trousers, so I'm your girl. Do you have any maybes as yet?'

'Not exactly. I have yet to venture inside.'

Adele turned to stare into the window at the shimmery, wispy, frothy frocks hanging off obscenely thin mannequins. 'Any reason you're looking in *this* particular window?'

'It's for Cameron's father's birthday.'

In the reflection Adele's eyes shimmied down a mannequin whose dress was low cut in places, high cut in others and barely worth putting on, it covered so little flesh. 'Happy birthday, Quinn.'

Rosie slapped her on the arm without even turning her head.

'Ow. So I take it you and the great and wondrous Camster are still on?'

'We're not *on*,' Rosie said, running her thumb hard down the middle of her palm to stop the tingle that had spread up her fingers at the memory of his hands touching her cheek, getting lost in her hair, stroking her naked back. 'We agreed that our relationship only extends so far as dining together on occasion, and now we are attending an event in tandem.'

Adele's eyes left the dresses to turn slowly her way. Her voice was impassive as she said, 'Heck, Rosie, I've never seen you so very giddy.'

Rosie squinted. 'I don't do *giddy*, and you know it. It's just new. He's different. And… Oh, shut up.'

Adele grinned. 'Mmm. Now he's invited you to his father's biggest-bash-Brisbane-has-ever-seen birthday party, where you will meet his whole family including his parents. Sounds ultra low key to me.'

Rosie scowled. 'Just help me find a dress.'

Adele's mouth quirked as she looked back at the window. 'Have you seen the price tags hanging off those there garments?'

Rosie shrugged. 'I can afford it.'

'That one costs as much as a small car.'

'There are side benefits to living in a caravan.'

'So it would seem.'

Rosie stared at a more demure black, shimmery sheath. It was beautiful. It was what someone who Cameron Kelly took to a party would be expected to wear.

She hadn't been kidding when she'd told Cameron how proud she was that he was going to face his dad. And she knew how hard it would be. She wanted to be there for him. And if she was truly honest the more she thought about it the more she wanted to be there, like she could somehow vicariously live through his experience now that it was too late for her to do the same with her own father.

And if that meant straightening her hair and pumping up her assets with chicken fillets, and stuffing herself into some dress that she'd never in a million years have picked out if she'd had the choice, could she do it? Should she do it? Was every new decision going to mean making room for him? Was it either do that or lose him?

'So, are we going in?' Adele asked. 'I'm fairly sure the sales assistant won't bring them out here unless you flash a platinum Amex.'

'Give me a minute,' Rosie said.

Adele rubbed a hand down her arm. 'Kiddo, you're starting to look a little flushed. Are you feeling quite yourself?'

And then it hit her.

She was as different as a person could be from the kind of date Cameron Kelly usually had on his arm at parties— She, in her unapologetic hand-me-down glory, with her *au naturel* hair desperately in need of a cut, and the big trap she couldn't keep shut. And he knew that.

Yet of all the women who would have jumped at the chance to be on his arm dressed in designer clothing, he'd asked *her*.

Rosie grabbed Adele's hand, tucked it into the crook of her arm and tugged her away from the shop window. 'I'm done here. We're going to the Valley.'

Adele tugged against her hand. 'No, Rosie! I'm not going to let you find some sad old second-hand prom dress to wear to Quinn Kelly's birthday bash. Please, for me, for the sake of the future princes of Brisbane you may one day be able to introduce me to, no!'

Cameron drove up Samford Road, one hand loosely working the steering wheel, the other running back and forth across his top lip.

Within hours he'd be face to face with his father for the first time since he was a teenager.

He could have given his mother a believable excuse. None of the family would have been surprised. But now that he'd committed he was not backing out.

A familiar National Park sign had him turning left towards Rosalind's. He breathed deep and pressed the accelerator to the floor. Even the whisper of her name helped relieve the pressure building inside his head.

Their night together had been beyond anything he could have expected. It was the most intense, affecting and wicked night of love-making of his young life. And right then he couldn't have been more impressed with himself for having had the mettle to go after her.

As he drove up her dirt driveway he was forced to slow, to shift his mind to focus on the matters at hand so that the low-hanging trees didn't scratch his car, and so he didn't land in the same great hole in the ungraded path in which he'd almost lost himself when he'd dropped her home the morning before.

That made it almost thirty-six hours since he'd last laid eyes on her, since he'd left her at the door of her crazy caravan, with its hills, sun and flowers painted all over the sides like some leftover relic of the seventies. Since he'd touched her hair, and held her tight, and kissed that spot on her lower back that made her writhe.

The tyres jerked against the wheel, and he concentrated fully on finding a path that led him to her door relatively unscathed.

The ground was dry, so his dress shoes didn't collect any mud as he picked his way up the path made only by her daily footsteps rather than by any kind of design.

He looked for a bell, but found nothing of the sort. At a loss for a moment, he lifted his hand to knock thrice on the corrugated door.

Shuffling was followed by a bump, then a muffled oath. Then, when she didn't appear in an instant, he tugged at his tie and hitched his belt so that it was perfectly set just below his navel. He straightened his shoulders and cleared his throat. He had no reason to be nervous. So why did he feel like he was seventeen again, and picking his date up for the senior dance?

The door whipped open, and that was where all fidgeting stopped.

Backlit by the warm, golden light of a small desk-lamp, and

helped along by the thin moonlight falling softly through the clouds above, Rosalind stood in the doorway looking like she'd stepped out of a 1930's Hollywood movie-set.

Her shoulders were bare, bar a thin silver strap angling across one shoulder. Lilac chiffon fell from an oversized rosette at her chest and swirled about her long, lean form like she had been sewn into it. Several fine silver bangles shimmered on her wrist. And her hair was pinned at the nape, with soft tendrils loose and curling about her cheeks.

He'd never once in his entire life been rendered speechless—not when one of his mates had streaked during the debate-team final. Not when he'd made a three-hundred percent profit on the sale of his first property. Not even when his father's only response to his declaration that he could never work for a man with so little backbone had been that, as long as he didn't work for the Kelly family, he was not welcome in the Kelly family home.

But Rosalind Harper, in all her rare, noble, charming loveliness, had him at a complete loss for words.

'Hi,' she said, her voice breathy, and he knew it had nothing to do with her rushing about before she opened the door.

She looked at him like she'd be happy to keep looking at him for as long as she possibly could. Like he was all she'd ever wanted, and all she would ever want.

His heart raced like a jackhammer. He felt the boundaries he'd set being smashed left, right and centre and he had no idea what to say, or do or think.

But then she let out a long, descending whistle and flapped her hand across her cheeks, and her eyes ran coquettishly down his dinner suit. His skin tightened every place her gaze touched, and his heart eased.

He snuck a hand to her waist, the fabric sliding against his palm until he connected with the curve of her hip. It took all of his self-control not to throw her over his shoulder, take her back inside her crazy home, close the door behind them and forget about the rest of the world.

Instead he leaned in and kissed her on the cheek, letting her sweet vanilla scent wash over him like a cure-all.

'You,' he said, his voice gruff, 'look like a dream. And that dress; there are quite simply no words.'

The smile he wrought lit her from the inside out. 'What,' she said, swinging from side to side, 'this old thing?'

Her tone was wry, but he knew she half-meant it. For nothing that romantic could ever have come from today.

'Are you ready?' he asked.

She held up two fingers. 'Two seconds. I'm still missing an earring. You'd think in a place this small that wouldn't be a concern, right?'

She turned and raced inside. He followed, intrigued at just how much Rosalind's home might reveal about the woman whose layers seemed to go on and on.

At one end an ajar door revealed the corner of a double bed which all but filled the space. It was covered in a soft, worn, pastel comforter. It was unmade. One pillow lay in the centre of the bed, dented where her head had lain. She was used to sleeping there alone. So far, the insights were entirely positive.

In the middle where he stood was the kitchen. He looked for photos of family or friends, but there were none on show. No knickknacks had pride of place on the pleasantly scuffed bench. It was almost as though she was on holidays rather than living in the place. He wasn't sure what to make of that.

He glanced up. In lieu of a chandelier was a home-made mobile of the solar system made from bent wire-hangers and string, planets made from chocolate wrappings, balls of rubber bands, and an old squash-ball pitted with teeth marks. He'd asked for insight and he'd been given a fanciful, inventive, dynamic mind. No surprise there.

He counted. No Pluto. Poor Pluto. He was in, then suddenly one day he was out. Cameron felt an affinity with the little guy. He only hoped Pluto was out there in the universe, kicking butt and taking names.

'Found it!' Rosalind called out from deep in the other end of the caravan.

In the bathroom, perhaps? He took a step in that direction, and out of the shadows a face peered back at him. Against one wall rested a life-size cardboard cut-out of a musclebound actor in a wetsuit. And just like that all the good the single pillow on her bed had done to his ego was wiped out. *By a piece of cardboard.*

He stepped back into the relative safety of the more conservatively decorated kitchen. His head brushed against something. He turned and came face to face with a line of string, over which had been hung a collection of skimpy lace underwear, quite different from the androgynous knickers she'd had on under her layers upon layers of clothing the other night.

He swallowed hard, wondering just what she might or might not be wearing under her diaphanous dress. The answer would be his for the taking if he wanted it, of that he was sure. And try as he might he couldn't imagine a situation in which he would not.

Before he had the chance to interpret the thought, Rosie appeared from the other end of the van, pinning the back on a dangly earring at her left lobe, saw where he was standing and came to a screeching halt. And blushed.

It wasn't even the loveliness of the blush that got him deep in his gut. It was the fact that, even after he'd already seen every inch of her beneath the underwear, she still managed to blush at all.

Their eyes caught. And locked. Her sparkling grey depths were warm, questioning, unguarded as always. But this time he felt like he was teetering on the edge of a most important discovery, when she closed her eyes and spun away, and it was gone.

'It's getting late,' she said, grabbing a clutch purse and a fake-fur wrap the same colour as her hair. 'Your family will be expecting you. How good does that feel?'

He let her lead the way, and paused when she simply shut the door and kept on walking.

'You're not locking up?' he asked.

She shot him a quick smile as she backed towards his car. 'No need. You met my faithful protector, didn't you? Serious eyes, big muscles, made of cardboard. He keeps me safe from harm.'

His eyes narrowed and he stalked to catch up. Not able to go even ten seconds without touching her, he slid an arm around her waist.

'Seriously,' she said, leaning away from him as though he was holding her as some form of punishment rather than for his own satisfaction. 'If anyone is brave enough to head into my woods at this time of night, they're welcome to whatever they find.'

When they reached the car he spun her to face him, holding her by the hips, his nostrils flaring as her sweet scent caught on the wind. 'Promise me when you come home tonight you'll lock that door behind you.'

Her eyes smiled. 'It's an old van. You can't open that front door unless you know exactly how to jiggle it. Nobody's getting in there, bar me or anyone I choose to let in.'

She kissed him on the lips, softly, lingeringly, with a promise he couldn't quite discern, then she slid into his car.

It took a moment for Cameron to collect himself before he rounded the back of the car, slid into the driver's seat and curled his way down her drive.

He kept half his focus on the road, half on preparing himself for the momentous evening ahead. Yet, even with all that to contend with, somehow he was never quite able to take his mind off the woman at his side.

By the time the front gates of the Kellys' family home loomed, Rosie was so nervous she could barely feel her toes.

Meeting the infamous Kellys was only half the problem. She was here for Cameron, and so long as she was herself and did her all to support him in his quest then she couldn't go wrong. But from the second he'd shown up at her door looking so suave, so sexy, so dark and delicious in his black tie, she had found it hard to remember how it was that she had promised him that she would be just fine when one day it all came to an end.

Cameron pulled up to the front gates, which opened in time for him to slide the car through. The charcoal-coloured driveway, embedded in a swirling pattern of white quartz, curled around a pristine green mound sprinkled with neat rows of white and orange roses.

Rosie pushed herself an inch off the seat. 'You have to be kidding me. Is that an Irish flag?'

Cameron didn't even need to glance at the garden to know what she was talking about. His mouth quirked into a smile. 'Welcome to Kelly Manor, where nothing is done by halves if it can be done twice as big.'

They drove on down the long, straight drive through an archway of oak trees which opened out to reveal a three-storey, dark brick, and cream trim, Edwardian-style home that looked like something out of an English period film.

Cameron pulled his car to a stop at the top of the circular drive. A liveried servant held the door open for Rosie, then took Cameron's keys in order to park the car goodness knew where, as the whole front drive was clear.

'Is this an intimate gathering?' she asked.

'Of course. Only a few hundred of my father's best friends.' There was no mistaking the tinge of bitterness in his voice.

She snuck her hand into the crook of his arm. 'You are doing the right thing. I meant it when I said if I had the chance to sit down and talk to my dad, to get things off my chest and let him explain himself in his own words, I'd take it.'

'You are a magnanimous woman, Rosalind Harper.'

'Well you, Cameron Kelly, are an amazing man. With a family who obviously want you to be a part of their lives. Don't blow it or I might never forgive you.'

'We can't have that, can we?' He tucked her hand close, and she could feel him drawing from her strength. It was a heady feeling indeed. One she found she liked very very much.

Fearing he might see in her eyes how much this was all affecting her, how much he was affecting her, she looked over her shoulder to find a Bentley cruising up the drive. 'This place is where the Thunderbirds got all their ideas, right?'

His laughter rumbled through her. 'Now what on earth are you talking about?'

'The cars. Where do they all go? I mean, the whole house opens up and there's an underground car-park beneath it all, right?'

Cameron unhooked her hand from his arm and snaked his arm around her hip as he guided her up the front steps. The move was possessive and sensual, sending her nerves spiralling up into the sky.

'You watch too much television,' he murmured against her ear, a wisp of hair tickling her cheek.

She leaned back into him. 'I work odd hours. I have an excuse.'

Cameron pressed the doorbell, and Rosie turned away to fix her hair, lick her top teeth in case of lipstick smudges and generally take in as much oxygen as she could before she entered the kind of rarefied air she had not had to endure since St Grellans.

'Everything okay?' Cameron asked, his hand touching her elbow in reassurance.

Over the top of the box hedges, Brisbane twinkled in the distance. 'Everything's fine. And for the record the view from your place is *way* better than this.'

Cameron grinned as the twelve-foot front door swung open, and he guided her inside. 'I knew I brought you for a reason.'

If the Kelly family had intended the front of their home to be imposing, it had nothing on the ballroom in which the party was being held.

Rosie's cold hands gripped the edge of a curling wrought-iron railing as she looked down from the gallery into the main room below.

Over two hundred people in evening dress milled about the massive rectangular space. A gleaming parquet floor shone in the light of six crystal chandeliers hanging from the multi-vaulted ceiling; a string quartet played in one corner of the room, a jazz band was setting up in the other, and white roses tumbled from every surface available.

She felt a sudden need to hitch up her dress.

'Come on,' Cameron said.

He took her hand and practically dragged her down the staircase and through the crowd so fast that he didn't have to stop and talk to anyone, and onto the dance floor, where several couples were swaying to the beautiful music.

He took her in his arms, pulled her close and together they danced.

With a blinding flash that had her losing her footing for a second, Rosie found herself deep in the middle of a memory she'd long since forgotten.

She was at the only school dance she'd ever attended. She'd been invited by a boy in her science class—Jeremy somebody. He'd been two inches shorter than her, and had always worn his trousers too tight, but in those days even to be asked…

Halfway through the night, dancing alone within the pulsating crowd, she'd turned to find herself looking into a pair of stunning blue eyes brimming with effortless self-belief. Cameron Kelly. A senior. She'd looked and she'd ached, if not to be with him then to be like him—content, fortunate, valued. He hadn't looked away.

And like that they'd danced with one another for no more than a quarter of a song before one of his friends had dragged him away for photos with the gang.

Cameron pulled her closer and drew her back to the present, just in time to hear him say, 'If only you'd let me dance with you this close all those years ago then who knows what might have happened?'

Rosie snapped her head back so fast she heard her neck crack. 'Excuse me?'

He pulled her back into his arms and wrapped her tighter

until her cheek was back against his chest, and she could feel the steady beat of his heart as he twirled her around the floor.

'My senior-year dance,' he said, the sound rumbling through her. 'You were there, weren't you?'

She closed her eyes lest he realise what she could no longer deny—that she was still very much the young girl with the naïve, wide-open heart that had seen something exceptional in him all those years ago.

'You remember,' she whispered.

'Mmm. I remembered a couple of days back, actually. I forgot to mention it til now.'

Her knees wobbled in recognition of the smile in his voice. Her poor, struggling heart wobbled right along with them.

'Skinny black jeans,' he continued. 'Hot-pink tank top, enough eyeliner to drown a ship. And I might be getting this part wrong, but did you have your hair in two long plaits?'

Rosie's hand lifted off his shoulder to slap across her eyes. 'Oh no, I'd forgotten that part. That was my "separate myself from the preppy, pastel suburban princesses before they separate themselves from me" phase. You know what? I'm not sure I ever grew out of that.'

Cameron slipped a finger beneath her chin and didn't slide it away until she was looking into his eyes. Those beautiful, corn-flower, soulful, sexy, smiling eyes. 'I'm glad. And for the record you looked adorable. And scary as hell.'

She blinked up at him, her brow furrowing. 'Scary?'

'God, yeah. I was mucking about, pretending to dance with my mates, and when I turned there was this stunning creature right under my eyes, chin up, eyes fierce, daring the world to even try telling her off for simply being herself. I was fairly sure that girl must have thought me ridiculous.'

'Ridiculous?' she repeated, beginning to feel like a parrot, but it was either that or say something she'd never be able to take back. That, in that moment, she'd been fairly sure she was looking at the most beautiful boy in the whole world.

She gripped his shoulder a tad too tightly, but he didn't seem to notice. He just looked deep into her eyes with that barely there smile lingering upon his mouth.

'It didn't take any kind of genius on my part to know you were far too cool for the likes of me.' He reached out and slid a finger under her fringe, pushing it off her face until he cupped her cheek. 'You know what? Nothing you've said or done this week has made me think any differently. Only now I'm old enough not to give a damn.'

And then he kissed her, so softly, so gently, her heart turned inside out.

'Well, if it isn't little Cam Kelly. I'm not sure I believe my own eyes,' a deep male voice drawled.

Rosie dragged herself out of the bottom of a beautiful dream and blinked into the warm light to find they'd stopped dancing.

And Cameron was no longer all hers.

His shoulders were stiff, his back straight, his neck tense as he stared at a taller man with slick hair and cold eyes.

'Brendan, this is my friend, Rosalind Harper,' Cameron said, his voice so cool if felt like the exhilarating warmth that had enveloped them both only moments earlier had all been in her imagination. 'Rosalind, this is my brother, Brendan. He is the heir apparent to my father's empire.'

Brendan gave her a short nod with a smile that didn't light his eyes. She smiled back and offered a tiny curtsy. His eyes narrowed, but his smile broadened, and Rosie caught a glimpse of Cameron's charisma therein.

'Which by the old joke makes our Dylan the spare,' Brendan said. 'And what does that make you, brother?'

'Delighted to be my own man.'

Feeling like she was in the middle of two lions circling one another, hoping to bite the other's head off, Rosie disentangled herself from Cameron's hold and waggled his little finger. 'I think I'll take a look around, see what there is to eat. Give you boys the chance to do what you need to do.'

'I'll come back for you soon,' Cameron said.

Rosie smiled, but a shiver ran down her back as she thought it would be asking too much to have the same good luck twice. 'Nice to meet you, Brendan.'

'Likewise,' he said, and this time she believed him.

As she walked away through a crowd of people she'd never met, and didn't particularly want to, she glanced back to find Cameron and his brother already deep in heated conversation.

She'd brought him here, she'd made his first step bearable. Was that as far as she was needed? She kept walking straight ahead and ignored the sadness that had once again begun to settle in her chest.

It was all she'd ever known how to do.

CHAPTER TWELVE

TEN minutes later Rosie leant against a marble column in the corner of the room, a champagne glass in one hand, a couple of *hors d'oeuvres* secreted within a linen napkin in the other. The food hadn't done much to ease the tightness in her chest; the champagne, on the other hand, had.

She watched Cameron and Brendan holding court with two politicians, a tennis pro and a guy with so many shiny medals on his chest she figured he was an army general.

For a guy who'd supposedly turned his back on all this guff, Cameron was in his element—while she was hiding lest she was forced to have another conversation about yachting, or golf, or the medical benefits of rhinoplasty.

'Rosalind Harper, right?'

Rosie blinked and spun to find Meg Kelly at her shoulder, her chocolate-brown curls bouncing about her perfect pink cheeks, and her petite figure poured into a glittery copper number that could not possibly have been worn as well by another living soul.

'Hey, Meg.' Rosie clamped her fingers around her glass to stop herself from checking her hair, from tugging at her dress, from feeling awkward and gangly and everything Meg Kelly was not.

'Having fun?' Meg asked.

'The mostest fun,' Rosie said. 'You?'

Meg's face twisted in the way that only someone who somehow knew she would never wrinkle could twist her face.

'I hate these things. So many ancient VIPs trying to kiss Dad's butt. I mean, if they had vodka cruisers rather than this dry, old champagne then maybe, just maybe, these nights might not make me feel so much like my youth is just slipping away. You know what I mean?'

Rosie sipped her champagne and smiled with her eyes.

'So how do your people celebrate birthdays?' Meg asked.

Rosie spluttered on her drink. 'My people?'

'Your friends and family.'

Rosie mentally kicked herself. Cameron was from *good* people. His friends were at heart good people. It stood to reason Meg would be good person too. Just because this night had wrenched up some latent feelings of inferiority and doubt, that wasn't her fault.

'Pizza,' Rosie said. 'Beer. Ten-pin bowling. Birthday cake with used candles. Pressies under thirty bucks a pop.'

'So, no ice-sculptures then?' Meg asked.

They both turned to look at the six-foot-tall melting bust of Quinn Kelly's head in the centre of the twenty-foot long head table.

'Ah, no,' Rosie said. 'Not that I can remember.'

'And don't you now think those parties were the poorer for it?' Meg's voice was deadpan, but her eyes were sparkling.

Yep, she thought, *Meg Kelly is one of the good ones*. She could barely imagine how hilarious she and Adele would be together.

'So,' Meg said, just as Rosie started to relax, 'You and my brother are together.'

'I think you'll find your brother is over there,' Rosie said carefully, 'While I'm over here.'

Meg tapped the side of her nose. 'I'm with you. Don't want to jinx things.'

Rosie made to correct Meg, but then realised she had no way of defining what they were that would make sense to anyone outside the two of them. Actually, the longer she spent alone, she was finding it hard to make sense of it herself.

Suddenly Meg stood straight as a die. 'Will you lookie there?'

Rosie's gaze shifted back to Cameron, to find that his father had joined the group, and her relationship with Cameron once again moved to the back of the line.

Her eyes darted between the two men. They seemed civil, at least from a distance. Profile on, they looked so similar— both tall, both straight-backed, both broad and ridiculously good-looking. Princes among men.

Only she knew Quinn Kelly was a man who liked to keep secrets. Secrets that could destroy those who loved him and needed him most. Secrets that had already destroyed that part of Cameron that was open to trust.

She had to loosen her grip on her champagne glass for fear it might smash in her hand.

All she could do was stand on the sidelines and wait. Wait for him to sort himself out. Wait for him to come back to her. The irony of her situation in comparison with her mother's wasn't lost on her. And the rest of her champagne was downed in three seconds flat.

'I truly never thought I'd see the day those two would manage to be in the same room together without shooting laser beams at one another with their eyes. Ever since Cam told dad he wasn't going to work for KInG, it's been the battlefield of Brisbane. What did you say to get him here?' Meg asked.

'Me?' Rosie said, lifting her napkin to the rosette on her chest.

'Yeah, you,' Meg said with a smile. 'It's only since you came on the scene that he's gone all soft and gooey around the edges. He called me twice this week. I don't remember a time he called me that often in a month!'

Rosie's stomach turned soft and gooey in half a second flat. But then she remembered that Cameron had not shared his fears about his father's health with Meg. It was more likely he'd been fishing and the timing had been coinciden-tal.

Then again, maybe not. Maybe the timing was everything. She stared into her champagne. Maybe everything in his life was backwards this week because of the situation with his dad.

An older couple who smelled of talcum powder and diamonds came wafting past, and Meg said just the right things to have them smiling and on their way.

'You make it look so easy—the schmoozing,' Rosie commented, her voice a tad breathless.

Meg sighed. 'I sing rock songs in my head, imagine them all wearing suspenders and fish nets and carry a flask wherever I go.'

She tapped her bag, which clunked with a metallic sound, patted Rosie on the arm, winked and boogied back into the crowd, air-kissing along the way until she found Tabitha, and then together they danced like they were at a rave.

But Rosie had the distinct feeling that Meg Kelly was no more the ditzy socialite she appeared to be than Cameron Kelly had been the carefree, lackadaisical golden boy she'd once thought he was. Or the dark, hard character she'd thought he'd turned into.

'What the hell is wrong with my brother, leaving you all alone in this crowd of vultures?'

Rosie turned to find Dylan Kelly leaning over her shoulder. She would have recognised him anywhere; he graced the social pages more than the rest of them combined. Fair, dashing, roguish, he grabbed her last *hors d'oeuvre* and popped it in his mouth.

'There is nothing wrong with your brother,' she said, snatching her near-empty champagne away lest he went for that too.

He grinned at her with his mouth full. 'Meg was right—soft and gooey. The both of you.'

'Sorry to disappoint,' she said. 'I don't have a gooey bone in my body.'

He leant against the side of the column, close enough for her to smell his aftershave. It was nice, but it was not Cameron. Just the thought of Cameron's clean, linen scent made her gooey, gooey, gooey.

'And what do you know of my brother's body?' Dylan asked.

'Are you absolutely certain the two of you are related?' she asked. 'Because I just can't see it.'

Dylan's laughter rang in her ears, and she wondered how Adele, Meg *and* Dylan would be in a room together. Add Tabitha, and it would be such a riot she'd be able to charge admission.

Her chest expanded expectantly at the thought that, if things continued to go well, her friendship circle could triple overnight. And all because Cameron had chosen to include her.

The second she had the chance, Rosie sought him out. To her eyes he stood out like a lantern on a foggy night. His dinner jacket was open, his left hand in his trouser pocket, his right hand lifting and falling as he told a story which held the group enthralled. Though his eyes never once touched on his father, who stood quietly to the side focussed completely on his youngest son, she knew Cameron knew he was there.

Dylan was mistaken; Cameron hadn't left her alone. She hadn't been rendered invisible once her work was done. She'd kept herself away, giving him the space she knew he needed.

Right?

Cameron's mind wandered, and not for the first time. Only once his gaze found Rosalind, and he knew she was being entertained—that she was smiling, happy and in safe hands—could he begin to relax.

Right now she was being entertained by Dylan, a guy he'd never been stupid enough to leave alone with a date even without the added benefit of trust issues. But seeing his brother with Rosalind...

Nothing.

It wasn't ambivalence he was feeling. Quite the opposite. He *knew* Rosalind was with him even when she wasn't with him. His trust in her was absolute. And, in a night filled with extraordinary moments, that was one of the more unexpected.

Dylan leant in close to her to point out something on the

ceiling. The guy took the opportunity to place a hand on her waist, feigning a need for balance.

And in the blink of an eye Rosalind had hold of the offending hand, bending his fingers back ninety degrees, and his brother was begging for mercy.

Cameron's first thought was, *that's my girl.*

That was the moment he felt his father slide in beside him.

'Nice girl,' Quinn said—the first words that had been spoken directly to him by the man in years. He couldn't have been less surprised.

'Nice doesn't even begin to cover it,' Cameron said, turning to look his father in the eye.

He looked older. Thinner. In person there was the same air of gravitas and power about him that there had always been. But he couldn't deny he'd seen what he'd seen, felt what he'd felt. There was no point in putting it off any longer.

'You're sick, aren't you, Dad?' His voice was dry. Emotionless. He had no idea how, as the words burned the inside of his throat as he said them.

'Wherever did you get that idea?' Quinn asked, smiling for his audience of hundreds.

'Dad,' Cameron pressed. 'Come on. This is me you're talking to—the one person on the planet who knows better than to fall for your line of bull. So tell me what's wrong?'

Quinn blinked at him as though not only seeing him for the first time in a decade and a half, but really *seeing* him for the first time.

'Nothing major. Just a couple of minor heart-attacks.'

Knowing had been one thing, having that thing confirmed was a whole other level of hell. Somehow he managed to keep his cool. 'How minor?'

'Minor enough I was able to call for Dr Carmichael myself when I felt them coming on. He brought me round both times without the need for anything so gauche as an ambulance. Just as well; those drivers would have sold some trumped up version of events to some shoddy paper within the hour.'

'So you've had no treatment apart from Dr Carmichael?'

'Not necessary.'

Cameron took a breath. 'Dr Carmichael is ten years older than you, and barely strong enough to hold a syringe, much less resuscitate a man your size.'

'Proving I was fine.'

'He has no other job but keeping you well. The guy wouldn't tell you it was serious for fear you'd fire him!'

'Which I damn well would. The man has no idea what a health scare would do to KInG. You, on the other hand, are smart enough to figure it out. So I trust you'll keep your concerns to yourself.'

Cameron scoffed. 'I've heard those words before.'

His father's face turned red, the kind of red that went with high blood pressure and too many whiskeys over too many years. Cameron's fingers stretched out to touch his arm, to stay him, to make sure he was okay—but Quinn jerked away as though one show of vulnerability would be enough to let the crowd in on the truth.

'Son,' he barked, 'It's not your secret to tell.'

'Well, then, that's a pity, because I've recently discovered the healing quality of letting secrets go.'

'Think of your mother,' Quinn warned.

Cameron got so close to his father he could count the red lines in the man's eyes. For that reason alone he kept his voice as calm as he could as he said, 'You're the one who needs to think of my mother a hell of a lot more than you ever do. I don't give a flying fig about the business, or the press, but I do care about the family. They may think you're a god, but I know that you are just a man. And I'm not keeping this secret—not from them—because if something happened to you and they didn't see it coming they'd never forgive you. So I'm back. Today's a new day for the Kelly clan.'

'Cameron?'

Rosalind's soft voice was enough to bring him off his high horse and back down to earth.

'Cameron?' she said again. 'I'm so sorry to interrupt, but Meg was looking for you. She needs you for a reason I can't mention in front of the birthday boy.'

Her hand clamped down on his forearm, gently but insistently. His vision cleared enough to tell him they had an audience. She'd just saved him from telling everyone in the room what even the family did not yet know.

Her other hand slid around his back, sliding along the beltline of his trousers, slow, warm, supportive. Vanilla essence, purely feminine warmth. Rosalind.

'Quinn,' she said, 'Happy birthday. And can I steal him away?'

His father nodded, then looked back to him, the slightest flicker of sadness damping his sharp, blue eyes before it disappeared behind the usual wall of invulnerability. But it was something. It was regret. It was a beginning.

'Happy birthday, Dad,' he said, leaning in to give his father a quick kiss on the cheek before turning and walking away.

'Oh God!' Rosalind whispered. 'I so apologise if that was the exact wrong moment, but you looked like you were about to bop him one. I thought you might need a distraction.'

The woman was a mind reader. He took a deep breath, wrapped his arm about her waist, leaned over and kissed the top of her head. 'Thank you.'

'For what?'

For what? For far too many things for him to extrapolate right now.

'Just thank you.'

'My pleasure. And your dad?'

He held her tighter and set his gaze straight ahead. 'I was right. Heart problems. Certainly worse than he is making out. The man simply won't admit weakness no matter what it costs.'

'And your family?'

'Know nothing. But not for long. I'll let them have tonight, but tomorrow I'll be back to tell them all. Give them the chance to make their peace.'

'Good man.'

Rosalind looked up into his eyes. She'd meant it when she called him a good man. And with it he felt the last of the places inside him that had been hard, fast and immovable for so very long melt away.

'Now Meg really *does* need you,' she said. 'Are you up for it? Whatever it is?'

'You bet.'

And as they joined his brothers and sister in an ante room he couldn't keep his eyes off Rosalind standing quietly in the doorway, watching the interplay between the four musketeers with a wistful smile on her face.

Tonight, rather than her distracting him from his family's dramas, his family's dramas had been distracting him from her. Being with her was where he constantly wanted to be. The words gathered in his throat, but not in any order he recognized, so he swallowed them back down.

'Cam!' Meg called out, clicking fingers in front of his eyes. 'Pay attention, Bucko, or I'll make you jump out of the cake instead of me!'

He blinked, then stared at his sister. 'You are not jumping—?'

'No.' She grinned. 'I'm not. But pay attention so we can get this done, and then, my little friend, the rest of the night is yours to do with as you please.'

He couldn't help himself. He looked to the doorway, only to find Rosalind had gone.

Happy Birthday had been sung by the world-famous St Grellans Chorale. A cake the size of a piano had been wheeled out by Quinn's four children, and a line of people had snaked around the room as everyone awaited their chance to get a piece of cake and slap some Kelly flesh.

Rosie stayed in the gallery, leaning on the railing and watching the proceedings from a more comfortable distance.

'You must be Rosalind.'

Rosie spun from the rail to find herself face to face with Mary Kelly, the matriarch of the Kelly clan, as petite as Meg, but overwhelming all the same—resplendent in a royal-blue gown, her ice-blonde hair swaying in a sleek bob. She was so elegant Rosie had to swallow down a raging case of stage fright.

And then the woman smiled, and Rosie knew where Cameron's natural warmth had come from. She couldn't help but smile right back.

She held out a hand. 'Rosie Harper. It's a pleasure to meet you, Mrs Kelly.'

'Rosie. Please, call me Mary.' Mary clasped Rosie's hand between both of hers. 'And the pleasure is all mine, I assure you. You're the girl who finally brought my Cameron home.'

Rosie realised how hard she was shaking her head when a lock of hair fell from her up-do and stuck to her lip gloss. She peeled it out as she said, 'Really, you've all got to stop saying that. I promise, it was all Cameron's idea, his attachment to you guys, that made him come. I was just the lucky girl who got a party invite.'

She could tell by the steely resolution in the older woman's eyes that she was having none of it. But before Rosie could press her case home—to somehow explain what they were, or maybe more easily what they weren't—Mary turned to glance out over the crowd, every inch a queen surveying her land and peoples.

'My Cam's always been a stubborn boy. He'd never accept help with his homework. Never come in from playing outside until he'd achieved whatever sporting milestone he'd set out to accomplish. He can want a lot from others, but is much harder on himself. Much like his father.'

Don't tell him that, Rosie thought.

'I'd never tell him that,' the woman said with an eloquent smile. 'Though it's why the two of them could never see eye to eye. They are both bull-headed. Determined. Competitive. Ambitious. And sadly unforgiving of human limitations.'

Rosie stopped nodding along when she hit the final word.

Her skin broke out in a splatter of goose bumps as the whole truth dawned: her husband's infidelity, his current illness, Mary Kelly knew it all.

What she didn't know was that her youngest son knew it all too. If she had, Rosie had no doubt she would have done everything not to let him suffer being an outcast to protect them all.

The fiercely independent side of her nudged her towards feeling sorry for the woman. But really Rosie just thought her immensely brave.

Mary Kelly's valiant choices had shaped four formidable children. Rosie had witnessed how naturally close they were in the ante room downstairs. If she'd still believed in wishing on a star, her wish would have been to be a part of that. To be able to tap into Meg's humour, Dylan's confidence, Brendan's strength, to be cushioned by that much unconditional devotion.

But she especially wanted to hug Mary Kelly for creating Cameron—a man who might well be bull-headed, but then so was she. While he was also gentle. Gentlemanly. Incredibly strong. Generous. Funny. Attentive. He had a huge heart and the soul of a dreamer.

Her cheeks began to warm. She'd never let herself list his good points in one go before, as though deep down she'd known that all together they would be overwhelming.

When she realised Mary Kelly was awaiting her response, she casually fanned her cheeks with her clutch bag as she said, 'Thank goodness for the renowned Kelly charm, then. I'd bet it gets them both out of a lot of trouble their mulishness gets them into.'

Mary smiled. 'Thank goodness for that. And for the fact that they are both men who have always known who they are. And what they want. That's a rare thing indeed.'

Rosie smiled back. All the while her mind spun and spun.

Cameron Kelly was a rare man. A man who worked hard and played hard, but above all wanted to be a good man. He *was* a good man. The best man. That such a man had pursued her, looked out for her, desired her, *needed* her…

And right there, standing next to Cameron's mother, it dawned on Rosie with the gently rising glow and warmth of a winter sunrise that it had taken a rare man to give her—a woman who had been certain that she would go a lifetime without knowing love—all the room she'd needed in order to know one thing with all her heart.

Rosie loved him. She was in love with Cameron Kelly. She loved him with a mad, aching, tumbling, soaring, absorbing, textured, lovely love.

Her lungs filled so deeply that the resultant burst of oxygen made her feel lightheaded, weak-kneed and tingly all over. Trying to find some kind of centre, she repeated the words over and over again in her head.

She loved him. She was in love with him. Rosie Harper loved Cameron Kelly.

After a while the words stopped making sense.

How could they? How could she have let herself love this man of all men? Cameron might have come here to broker a peace, but the cuts from his father's betrayals ran deep. They had screwed with his sense of gallantry so much that, even if a miracle occurred and he ever came close to loving her back, his critical fear of hurting those he loved would be one great reason for him to let her go.

That was what he'd been trying to tell her that night after the Chinese at his place. He'd been warning her. Subconsciously he'd seen this coming, even if she had pretended she was fine.

Her flutter of instinct when she'd been with Meg had been spot on. While Cameron had thought he'd found himself an easygoing girl who would know better than to fall for him, Rosie had gone against character and done just that.

She'd fallen head over heels in love with the one man who could never be hers.

Punch drunk, Rosie inhaled deeply, but this time the air

felt like it barely touched her lungs. There were too many people. Crowding into her personal space. Making it impossible to breathe.

'It's been lovely to meet you all, Mrs Kelly. You have an amazing family,' she managed to get out without choking. 'Please excuse me.'

She blindly stumbled onto one of a dozen half-circle balconies leading off the gallery, towards fresh air. And open sky.

Looking up into the infinite stars—all of them seemingly serene and quiet, yet crashing, imploding, living and dying out of control right before her eyes—she managed to get air into her lungs once more.

Cameron leant in the frame of the balcony doorway, watching Rosalind.

Her hair flickered in the soft breeze. Her dress clung to her subtle curves. His blood warmed as he imagined wrapping himself about her again tonight. Celebrating with her. Taking her with him to the heights he was feeling, and finding solace in her arms as he came to terms with his father's mortality. And his own.

Her long, lean fingers gripped the columned balustrade, her eyes looking up.

That was one of the many things that drew him to her: her restless energy. She was hard to satisfy. He felt exactly the same way. At least, he had for years.

But looking at her now, her delicate shoulders braced to take on whatever her stars might throw at her, he felt something inside him shake free and settle.

The three steps that took him to her felt like they took an eternity. He slid his arms around her waist, leant his chin on her shoulder and kissed the tip of her ear.

She melted against him, a perfect fit, and he felt her whole body sigh.

But then her hands clasped down on his; she peeled his hand away from her waist and stepped away.

She glanced at him from beneath her lashes, and he realised she was upset. Soft swirls of wet mascara bore witness to the tracks of her tears.

His fists clenched, ready to take on Dylan or Meg or Brendan or whoever had said something to make his big, brave girl so distressed.

He went to touch her again. 'Rosalind, honey…'

She held up a hand, and he stopped mid-step.

'What's wrong?' he asked.

'I can't do this any more,' she whispered between her teeth.

'Do what?' he asked. But while his fists unclenched all of the newly settled places inside him began to squeeze in expectation.

'This.' Her arms flew sideways, taking in the balcony, the ballroom, the immaculate grounds.

'Fine,' he said. 'I've done what I came here to do. Why don't we go home?' He wasn't sure where that would be, his place or hers, but as long as she was with him he didn't really much care.

He reached out to take her hand, which even in the beginning had always felt like the most natural thing in the world. But she pulled her hand away as though burnt.

'I can't,' she croaked. 'No more. Enough is enough.' Two fat tears slid down her blotchy pink cheeks. She swiped them away in frustration. 'Why did you even bring me here?'

He opened his mouth to tell her, then realised what a complicated question that really was. Less than a week earlier she'd been a welcome distraction. But tonight…

'This was always going to be a difficult night, and knowing you were here with me, for me, made all the difference. I could never have done this without you.'

He took another step. She shook her head so hard her curls drooped.

Realising she was more than upset—she was so distraught he wasn't sure she even heard him—he thought harder, went deeper. 'Asking you to come was not a decision I made lightly.'

Her eyes were like chipped ice when she looked up at him. 'Neither was my agreeing to come.'

He slid his left foot back to meet his right, keeping space between them while he tried to figure out what was happening.

It had all seemed to be going so well. Meg thought her fun, Dylan thought her hot, she'd earned his father's respect in an instant, and his mother had merely kissed him on the cheek and smiled, which told him everything. What had happened during *Happy Birthday*?

'Rosalind, I'm sorry, but I'm at a loss as to what's going on here.'

'It's *Rosie*,' she shot back. 'Just plain old Rosie. Which is exactly why you asked me here. But that doesn't make me some oddment you can flash about to get a rise out of your father. Or a diversionary girl to get Meg and Dylan off your back. Or a false hope for your mum. That's just not cool. I don't deserve that.'

She was so upset her voice was catching on her words, as though she could scarcely draw breath. It physically pained Cameron not to gather her up in his arms and make everything better.

But the truth was she was spot on—from the beginning he'd used her. Even when he'd realised she was too smart, too clued into him, not to figure it out. Now he'd hurt her when he'd promised himself he would never hurt anyone he cared for.

His only chance was to show her, and himself, that deep down he wasn't the cold, calculating man he'd been acting like for the past week.

'This has been a night for fresh starts,' he said. 'Maybe we could take a leaf out of that book and try for one ourselves.'

She laughed, but it was tinged with bitterness, the likes of which he'd never felt from her. He felt it like a slap across the face.

She said, 'You are on a high, and I get that. I am honestly so happy for you that you have that. But let's be honest— you've never pretended that you had any intention of committing further time and energy to this than you absolutely had to. Don't start messing with me now.'

God, but the woman was stubborn! His hands clenched into fists rather than reaching out and shaking her. 'You want me to be brutally honest?'

His frustration came through his voice. She glanced up at him, her eyes like silver charms in the moonlight.

'Why the heck not?' she said.

'Fine. Then here it is. You are honestly the most difficult, defiant, demanding woman I have ever met. And I think you ought to try to find it in you to give me a break. Now, do you really want to talk about commitment?'

'Yeah. Let's.' She crossed her arms and glared at him. She was so fierce it brought about a growl deep down inside his chest. He would have grabbed her and kissed her had it not been for the fact that she was driving him so damned crazy.

He said, 'As far as I can tell, apart from some far-away planet that can't answer back, you've never committed to a thing! Not to a job that isn't freelance. Not to a home that you can't up and move with an hour's notice. Not even to your own name.'

The heat in her eyes made his lungs burn as he breathed deep to keep from saying any more; his skin felt a hundred degrees. And he'd never been so turned on in his whole life. Not by success, or power, or by being the one man in town gutsy enough to build the tallest, greatest, most spectacular buildings his city had ever seen.

'Fine,' she shot back. 'If I'm the world's greatest hypocrite, then you are the most wilfully pig-headed man in the universe. Do you have any kind of clue what you have? You are surrounded by people who love you so much.' Her eyes flickered from his for a moment before slamming into him again. 'Family who need you, who want you in their lives no matter what. You have roots in this place a mile deep, and you've done everything in your power to chop them off. One of these days they might not grow back, then you'll have the faintest clue what it truly feels like to be alone in the universe.'

Two fat tears slid from her eyes and peeled pathetically down her cheeks. The ache it created inside him knocked him sideways. He wished he knew how to tell her. He wished she would let him hold her, kiss her, show her, so that he didn't have to find the words—as he wasn't even sure he knew what the words should be. But she let him off the hook by staring hard at her shoes.

'Can you please thank you mother for a lovely party? Give my regards to the rest.'

She looked up and captured his eyes with hers. He felt like his whole life had led him to this one minute in time. The defining minute of his life. Was he really a good man after all? Would a good man get on his knees and tell her how he felt, or would a good man realise he'd hurt the woman enough and let her go?

All of a sudden an explosion of sounds startled them both rigid. A half-second later fireworks burst and sparkled in the sky over the river.

The balcony quickly became crowded with guests, oohing and ahhing, and Cameron felt Rosalind being tugged from him. It wasn't until he lost her within the sea of faces that he realised she'd been the one doing all the tugging.

Suddenly she was gone.

And, though he was surrounded by people, including the family he'd taken back into his life this night, he already felt more alone than he'd even known it was possible to feel.

CHAPTER THIRTEEN

CAMERON had ditched his jacket and tie, his sleeves were rolled up past his elbows, his forearms leant against the cold stone of the ballroom balcony and he watched blue turn to pink as morning came round.

Venus was already up, steadfast in the sky. Unlike the other heavenly bodies that had set with the moon, there was no unsteady flickering, no distracting twinkling. She was constant, unwavering, enchanting and all alone.

Something hard and heavy thumped behind his ribs, and not for the first time in the past twelve hours. In fact, the thumping and heaviness had come over him the moment Rosalind had left him standing in this exact place.

The hours had passed. He and his family had retired to the library once all the guests had gone, and he had told them all about Quinn's heart attacks and stubborn refusal to seek treatment, and together they had fought, reconciled, laughed and cried—and he'd come to realise that he'd never in his life been really alone.

But Rosalind had—solitary in her work, isolated in her home, alone even in her family. And it didn't matter any more that she might have done everything in her power to keep at arm's length those things that could provide her the same easy comfort he'd enjoyed; he finally understood the reason.

Loving something, then losing it, hurt like hell.

Was she out there hurting right now? Hurting and alone, because of him? Because he'd been too stubborn, too scrupulous, too disenchanted to take on the mess that came with the good in any real relationship?

A good man would suck up his pride, put himself in the unpleasant position at being rejected twice in twenty-four hours and do what he had to do to to make sure the person he cared about knew she would never have to be alone again.

He glanced at his watch. The hour was nearly polite enough. Home, a shower, a change of clothes; he pushed himself upright, stretched his tight arms over his head then felt in his pocket for his car keys.

If she slammed the door in his face afterwards, he'd never darken her door again. If her eyes confirmed how deeply he believed she cared, if she opened the door wide and let him in…

The rush of his next thought was stripped from him as a hard hand slapped down upon his shoulder. Dylan sidled in beside him, dressed much the same way as Cameron since none of them had yet been to sleep.

'So this is where you've been hiding since the big brouhaha?' Dylan said.

Cameron slapped a hand around his brother's shoulder and turned them back inside. 'You know as well as I do there are far better and darker places to hide in this monstrosity than on an open balcony.'

Dylan grinned. 'I'm thinking right about now Dad would pay good money to know just one.'

They meandered through the upper level, gravitating towards the kitchen as they had a thousand times before. It didn't feel like he'd spent years away from this place. It just felt like home.

And there was one person he had to thank for showing him the way back. He glanced at his watch again, restlessness beginning to take hold.

Dylan held open the swinging door of the massive white-and-wood kitchen, but not quite so far that Cameron could slip through.

His dress shoes came to a squeaking halt, and he looked up at his brother in time for Dylan to say, 'Thanks, mate.'

'For what?'

'For opening our eyes. For not letting the old man twist your arm. For giving us all the chance to remind him that he was the one who always told us to put family first, and it's about time he remembered that. It's tense in there right now, but once everyone calms down they'll realise the air in this place has never seemed so clear.'

Dylan let the door swing closed to give him a hug. Cameron hugged back, wondering how the hell he'd forsaken this all these years. Not for one more day would he forsake his own happiness for the sake of some cold, loveless principle.

When Dylan let him go and headed into the kitchen, Cameron looked to his watch again. It was nearly seven. She was a morning bird; she'd be up.

Not for one more day? He wasn't going to deny himself the chance at happiness another minute.

Dylan grabbed a slice of birthday cake and a glass of milk from the fridge. 'You staying for breakfast?'

Cameron shook his head, his mind a million miles away from there already. 'Not this time.'

'Damn it. I was itching to find out what new bombshell you might drop over waffles—Brendan's gay? Mum voted Labour? Meg's adopted, as she always hoped? No? Fine; so what *are* your plans for this fine day? Tell me they involve that fabulous young thing who accompanied you here last night and I might forgive you.'

Cameron took a swipe of icing. 'I have high hopes.'

Dylan paused. Then said, 'How high, exactly?'

'Ridiculously, I'm afraid.'

'Do tell.'

'She accused me lately of having no staying power, and I am of a mind to prove her wrong.'

'Wow. Don't tell me you're in need of the little blue pills yet? You're younger than me.'

Cameron elbowed his brother neatly in the solar plexus and was rewarded with a satisfying, 'Oomph!'

He slipped the icing into his mouth, and the sweetness exploded on his tongue. Then he said, 'Rosalind knew I was making excuses. What I didn't realise was that with her I didn't need to.'

'She's figured you out, then?'

Cameron breathed in deep through his nose. Then he pushed away from the island to head to the door leading outside, to his car, to her. 'That she has.'

'Excellent,' Dylan said with a chummy grin. 'It seems I may have a bombshell to drop over breakfast after all.'

Rosie sat on Adele's couch, staring unseeingly at the shifting yellow stripes on the wall left by the early-morning sun spilling through the wooden blinds behind her. Her feet were tucked beneath her, her legs covered in the blanket beneath which she'd slept—kind of. A bit. Not really.

In fact she'd been awake pretty much all night having deep and meaningful conversations with herself across a range of matters that had all led back to the one crucial fact: that she had gone and done the most stupid thing she could ever do and fallen for Cameron Kelly.

About three minutes after the cab had pulled out of the Kelly Manor driveway, the words, 'Turn this cab around right now!' had crowded her throat. Shouldn't she at least have allowed herself the chance to be loved back?

A deep breath, a sharp tug of the hair at the back of her neck and an extra five kilometres distance, and she'd been certain that she'd been on the verge of unashamedly setting herself up for heartache again, and again, and again…

Repeat one-hundred times, and that had been her night.

Adele came into the lounge with a tray of coffee, cake, chocolate, salt-and-vinegar chips, and lollies in the shape of milk bottles.

'How you doing, snook?' Adele asked, pouring her a strong cup of coffee.

'Better.' She uncurled her legs before they got stuck that way, and let her toes scrunch into the coarse, woven rug at her feet.

Adele's eyebrows rose. 'All better?'

Actually she felt like a walking bruise. She wrapped her hands around the hot mug and glanced at Adele over the top. 'Thanks for letting me stay.'

Adele blinked down at her several times before saying, 'Thank me later.'

Then the doorbell rang.

Adele jumped. She glanced at the door, back at Rosie, then back at the door. She said, 'I think I left the iron on. Can you get that?' And then shot from the room.

The doorbell rang again.

Rosie dragged herself from the couch, ran fingers through her thicket of hair, rubbed her hands hard over her face to make sure all the bits were where they were meant to be and trudged to the door in her borrowed pyjama bottoms, T-shirt and bare feet. The delivery guy would just have to suck it up and pretend she didn't look like a one-woman freak show.

She hauled open the door and found herself face to face with a crumpled khaki shirt with rolled up sleeves, revealing the greatest pair of forearms God had ever created. And on the end of them...

'Cameron!'

'Hi,' he said.

She swallowed. It seemed his name was the most she could hope to say.

His hand reached up to cup the doorframe, as though she might be about to slam the door in his face—like he couldn't see that her irrational heart was trying its best to leap from her chest and into his beautiful arms.

'Can I...?' He cleared his throat. 'Rosie, can I come in?'

Rosie… Had he just called her Rosie?

She curled her toes into the hard wood and, no matter how hard she tried to resist, all the stagnant, decided places inside her began to flutter back to life. Which was ridiculous. He was likely there because she'd left something behind, and he was so damned civilised he was returning it by hand.

Needing an anchor, someone on her side, she glanced over her shoulder but there was no sign of Adele.

Then he said, 'I tried calling you last night. Many, many times.'

She closed her eyes, swallowed hard then looked back to him. His hair was mussed. His jeans unironed. Stubble shadowed his jaw. She'd never seen him so sexily rumpled.

She licked her dry lips and tugged at her T-shirt, and amidst the fidgeting it occurred to her that beneath the sex-god rumples he also looked tired, grey around the eyes, like he hadn't had much in the way of sleep either.

Her hand shook and she gripped her T-shirt tight. 'I left my mobile at home.'

A crease came and went in his cheek. 'I managed to somehow convince myself of that after the first dozen times you didn't answer. So I called Adele. She told me you were here. That you were still…upset. And that I should give you time.'

Rosie glanced at the angle of the sunlight on the porch outside. 'It can't yet be eight o'clock.'

He didn't even need to look to his watch before he said, 'It's not.'

She blinked at him once, then turned and walked inside. The soft click of the door told her far less than her next breath, which was filled with his clean, male scent.

Her knees wobbled plenty before she plopped back onto the couch. Cameron sat next to her. Close. Her scrunched-up blanket had the other third all to itself.

'Rosie—'

'Coffee?' she asked, her voice overly loud. She as yet needed time to collect herself. To protect herself.

He nodded. She poured.

'I'm not sure where Adele has gone; she was here a minute ago.'

'She gave me a goodbye wave over your shoulder when I first arrived. I'm assuming this place has a back door.'

Rosie swallowed hard. And nodded. They were alone. She would have no choice but to anchor herself.

He said, 'I'll get straight to the point, then, shall I? Which would be a first, I'm sure. We do seem to have an uncanny ability to lay things on the line without ever really getting to the point of what we are trying to say.'

Her hand shook. She stopped pouring halfway, lest she end up with more scars for her troubles. Then she pushed a mug in front of him, but his hands remained clasped on top of his thighs.

He waited til she looked him in the eyes, those deep, dark-blue eyes, now so solemn, so serious. She nodded. She was as ready as she'd ever be.

'So, last night on the balcony, you accused me of not appreciating what I had. And I want you to know that I think you were absolutely right.'

Rosie swallowed. This was not what she had expected at all.

He went on, 'I've put so much time and effort into my work, and my home, the parts of my life that don't offer any form of opposition. And not because it was right, but because it was easier than facing the truth—that I have been taking for granted those things which should have been more important the whole time.'

As he spoke, as he confessed, his stunning, searching, blue eyes never once left hers, not a for a second. If she had an ounce of faith left in her judgement she might have fancied he was talking about her. But that boat had sailed the minute she'd said yes to a date with a guy no sane woman could know and not love.

Needing a distraction, she grabbed a handful of milk-bottle lollies and nibbled on the end of one. His gaze finally left her eyes and rested on her lips before they slid back up.

He rolled his shoulders once, then continued. 'I thought my

life was good. But now I see that it was completely untethered, all the separate parts unconnected, because I was afraid that I might one day slip up, word would get back and my family would be hurt. Then you came along, and I slipped. Over and over again. And you know what?'

'What?' she asked, her chest lifting as she breathed in deep.

'The world didn't end. And last night I began the process of joining the dots. I have reconnected with old friends. I have spoken with my father. I have my family back.'

She smiled a wobbly smile. Because she was happy for him. She really was. Not so happy for herself...

Until a hand reached out and took hers, its fingers curling around hers until they were indelibly knotted together. Reconnected.

'Rosie,' he said, and her heart beat so hard she heard it in her ears. She lifted her eyes to see that he was smiling too. 'Sweetheart, the glue that brought it all together was you.'

Her heart rate had nothing on the blood rush to her head. She shook it to try to clear the haze, to pick out the truth from the hope that was blurring everything. 'I'm not glue,' she said. 'I'm the opposite of glue. I don't even have any dots to join. You said it yourself—I work freelance, I live in a van, there is nothing in my life I couldn't walk away from given a moment's notice. I know nothing about being glue. All I do know is that the easiest way to break a person's spirit is to take away the things they love. I didn't want that to happen to you.'

'You were too late. It already had. But look at me. I'm still here.'

Cameron was still there, the strength of his spirit radiating from every pore. 'So here's what I think about all that—a spirit can be broken only if it's prone to breaking in the first place. And Rosie, honey, you are a force of nature. Your spirit is so vibrant, so fresh, so honest, I am certain there is nothing in this world that could ever break you.'

She blinked hard, then down at their entwined hands. It was true, her spirit still raged inside her even after the night she'd had.

She felt sorry for her mum, angry at her dad, proud of Cameron. So she might not be broken. But that didn't mean that the cracks didn't feel like they were being held together with old gum.

'Cameron—'

'Cam,' he said, cutting her off. 'Those closest to me call me Cam.'

Her eyes were drawn back to his like magnets to steel. His smile remained, urged her to really listen. He was telling her that she was his glue. That he considered her a person close to him. That, even after she'd run scared the night before, he was still here.

Rosie felt the moment heave between them, draw breath and wait. Her world, her universe, her past, present and future felt as though they were teetering on her next words.

'Cam,' she said on a release of breath—and the smile that had been hovering on the corner of his mouth broke free, beaming as bright as morning sunshine, until all she could do was bask in the glow.

'Yes, Rosie?'

'Actually,' she said, 'I don't so much mind if you call me Rosalind.'

His brow furrowed, and she didn't blame him. She wasn't sure where she was heading either. Her mind was a blank page, untinged by history or expectation. All she could do was anchor herself in the warmth of his hand wrapped around hers and give him as good as he'd given her.

She snuck a foot beneath her and faced him. 'I am Rosie. Rosie who camps out in a van, loves comfortable boots, clothes with a past, and sleeps when regular sorts are awake and vice versa. But since I met you…'

Her voice caught.

'Since I met you, Rosalind—the girl I was, the version of myself I kept at bay all these years—came back. That part of me craved affection, wanted nothing more than to feel special, wanted to know what it was like to be the centre of someone's attention. Rosalind isn't afraid to hope.'

His other hand lifted off his thigh. She held a finger near his lips. He held his breath and stared at it. Though she had no idea what was coming next, all she could do was let the flood of words carry her til she found land.

'Since I met you, since I met your friends and your family, I finally knew what it must be like to have kinship—be a part of a collective spirit, of something enveloping, warm, vital. Watching you, Meg, Dylan and Brendan mucking about with your dad's cake, I would have given my left leg to have been allowed into that inner sanctum for just one more day. I hope you understand, I had to, *have* to, walk away. Taking it away from me any later would have been too much to ask.'

'Who's asking?' he asked, his voice deep, warm, encouraging.

Then the edge of his mouth kicked up into the whisper of a smile. His thumb found her palm and began running up and down the centre, sending goose bumps all around her body, inside and out.

She closed her fingers around his thumb and twisted it away. 'I… I'm not exactly sure what you're intimating. In all honesty, I'm kind of hazy about a lot of things right now. I've been up all night. I'm wearing someone else's pyjamas. I haven't showered.'

He took her hand back in his, turned it over and pressed his warm lips upon her palm. 'You smell great.'

A slow build of warmth settled low in her stomach. 'I smell like milk-bottle lollies and mothballs.'

'You smell like you.'

The warmth began to seep into her limbs, into her head, giving her ideas that maybe, just maybe, the only thing she'd left behind at the party had been him.

'Cameron,' she breathed.

He held up a finger to her lips, not stopping short, letting the calloused tip brush against her soft mouth.

'Rosalind,' he said, her name rolling off his tongue as poetically as it was meant to be. 'One of the many things I have long since found so irresistible about you is that, while you are such a champion of human frailty, you are determined to deny your own.'

'I don't. I—'

'Shush. Really. For your own good. It's my turn again.'

He took a deep breath and let it out through his nose, and Rosie realised that he wasn't just tired—he was nervous. He was wide open and unguarded. She opened her ears and listened.

'The night I suggested we slow things down…' He waited for her to nod along, his hand again holding hers tight. 'I was following a pattern I had followed time and time again. A whiff of getting too close, I put on the brakes. But when you left I realised it wasn't you getting too close that panicked me, it was *me*. It was so unanticipated that I took a long, hard look at my life without you in it and I didn't much care for what I saw.'

Just to make sure she was right there with him, he reached out and cupped her cheek. But she was there; she was all there.

'I had thought heading into the bush in the middle of the night to find you was enough of an admittance of my feelings, and that all I had been trying to do was protect you from every possible harm, including myself. I look back now and wonder what time and anguish I could have saved had I just had the guts to tell you straight. Like last night…' His eyes burned, as though he'd been sliced with a red-hot poker. 'I should never have let you walk away before we'd managed to have this exact conversation. Thankfully this week I've learnt not only how easy it is for all men to make mistakes, but how easy it can be to forgive them.'

He slid his hand into her hair, caressing her ear, drawing her closer. His beautiful blue eyes smiled into hers. Her heart danced. Her liver forgot itself. And the rest of her insides skipped and tumbled, and hoped more than they'd ever hoped in their life.

'Forgive me,' he asked.

Her voice shook when she said, 'I never gave you a chance. Forgive *me*.'

He slid his hand into her hair, drawing her closer. 'Since we are both extremely adept at complicating the heck out of everything, how about I try something new and make things really simple?'

'It's worth a try.'

'Rosalind,' he said, his voice almost as shaky as hers. 'My Rosie. I need you to know that I am very much in love with you. That I have loved you for some time. And I have no doubt that I will love you as long as I can draw breath.'

The second he'd said her name, warm tears streamed down her face, but she couldn't possibly lift a hand to wipe them away. She thought she might have to resort to using a shoulder when Cameron leaned in and kissed them away, one side then the other.

Before things kept moving in the direction it was obvious they had to, she stilled him with a hand at his chest. She looked from one eye to the other, until she was certain she had his attention completely. 'Last night, watching you wield the kind of strength that most men don't even know is possible, I knew I loved you too.'

His eyes glinted, his chest swelled, and the hand in her hair drew her in. 'Funny way you had of showing it,' he murmured.

'As it turns out, I am a funny girl.'

He grinned. 'Lucky me.'

And then he kissed her. She melted into his arms as he pressed her back against the couch. Her delighted hands slid up the back of his shirt, her legs entwined with his, and she kissed him until she saw stars; she was lost. Wholly and completely and beautifully lost. The sensation filled her, overwhelmed her, and didn't scare her in the least.

For she had not actually lost something, she'd finally found herself again in him.

Eons later, when they pulled apart, Rosie's lungs burned, her lips were hot and swollen and her whole body felt heavy and languid. Cameron on the other hand had admirable strengths. He lifted her back upright until she was sitting across his lap.

His sexy eyes narrowed as he asked, 'You did say that you loved me, right? That was one hell of a kiss, and could have been enough to have made me imagine it.'

'I do love you,' she repeated, the liberation of the words, of the feeling, of what it would bring her, making her feel sky high.

'Excellent,' he said. 'Then, before we go ahead and christen Adele's couch, I have one more thing I have to get off my chest.'

Rosie pushed a scruff of hair off his forehead, and allowed herself the crazy luxury of playing with his hair. 'This is *really* not the moment to confess you have a secret love of boy bands. Or that you already have three wives and they're all called Rosalind. And there is no way I'm ever giving up my cardboard cut-out; he was a gift, and is a collector's item, so—'

'Rosie.' His eyes narrowed, but the sexy grin that accompanied it only made her want to curl up and purr. 'You're going to have to answer your phone when I call.'

She blew a raspberry, and continued playing with his thick, beautiful hair. 'That's asking too much.'

He pointed a finger at her nose. 'If I have to call Adele every time I want to see you or talk to you, or tell you I love you, or when I get the sudden urge to talk dirty to you in the middle of the day when I'm all hot and sweaty at the work site and you're wrapped up snug under your comforter in bed, then I guess that's how it's going to be. It's you, me and Adele for ever.'

The hot and sweaty talk had her turning her attentions to the top button of his shirt. 'Or…?'

He reached round behind him and pulled out a small silver box wrapped in a big white bow. She'd been so caught up in the fact that he was there at all, she hadn't even noticed him bring it inside.

'For me?' she asked.

He nodded.

She opened the box, realising she had no clue what kind of gift a man like him, a man who knew everyone, who could get his hands on anything, would…

'Oh, Cameron.'

On a bed of soft silver paper lay a mobile phone. It wasn't gleaming, new, expensive, complicated and demanding—it was simple, easy, and just retro enough for her to fall in love with it in a heartbeat.

She ran her fingers over the big, bumpy buttons. 'Oh Cameron, she's beautiful.'

He slid the phone from her hand and she whimpered. 'What's beautiful about it,' he said, ignoring her, 'is that I've programmed it already with all the numbers I could think of that you might need in the near future.'

She snuggled in beside him so they could look at her beautiful new-old phone together. 'Show me.'

He showed her. 'There's the planetarium's number. Adele's. I tracked down the number for your supervisor in Houston.'

Rosie lifted her head to stare at him.

'I had many hours to kill last night, remember.'

His cheeks pinked—tough, sharp, skyscraper builder Cameron Kelly pinked—then dragged her back into his arms.

'Meg, Dylan, Brendan, and my parents are all there.'

She blinked. It was as if he'd known how much that would mean to her. It was as if he knew her better than she even knew herself.

'And last but not least,' he said, 'Press the one button then send.'

She did, and up came the first number on her speed dial. His mobile number, and the name *Cam*.

No fanfare. No dibs on himself. No Mr Cameron Kelly, esquire, builder of skyscrapers, Prince of Brisbane. Just her self-assured guy who knew her and loved her, and wanted to be the first person she'd ever think to call.

Rosie looked up at him and said the first words that came to mind. 'Will you marry me?'

He tilted his head to kiss her, slow, soft, deep, for ever, before saying, 'It would be my pleasure. How does tomorrow sound?'

She smiled against his lips. 'Fabulous. But I'm sure we have to register, and it takes like a month in case we change our minds, and—'

'First, I'm not changing my mind. Once I commit to something, that's it. And, more importantly, I'm a Kelly. I can do whatever I want.' He grinned. 'I knew one day that would come in handy.'

She moved to kiss him some more, but he edged back.

'One problem. You're going to have to get a bigger caravan. I've seen your current bed and I'm far too big for it.'

'That's okay,' she said, turning away to bury her head into his shoulder while she scrolled through her chunky phone's limited options. 'I don't think I can live another winter in the van now that I know all about that fireplace in your house. Even if you'd said no to marrying me, I was thinking about squatting. The place is so big you might never have noticed.'

Cameron grabbed her phone and threw it on the far sofa, where it bounced once and landed face up on a cushion.

'Well, thank God you did that,' she said, turning into his arms to kiss him. 'I didn't have the heart.'

The next time she came up for air, Cameron looked so deep into her eyes she felt like she could happily drown in them.

'I promised myself,' he said, 'if you turned me away at the door today I'd let you go. But I was kidding myself. If you'd slammed the door in my face I would have climbed through the window, down the chimney, up a drain pipe, to get to you. Not because I'm used to getting my way, but because I can no longer picture my way without you there beside me.'

'That's lucky. Because that's right where I plan to be.'

Air was overrated, Rosie thought as she settled back into his embrace. Kissing Cameron was not.

By the time Adele got home an hour later, the house was

empty. And the two full coffee cups were on the coffee table. Unnoticed, untouched.

It seemed the couple they were meant for had been far too distracted to remember anything but one another.

* * * * *

*Celebrate 60 years of pure reading pleasure
with Harlequin!*

To commemorate the event, Harlequin Intrigue® is
thrilled to invite you to the wedding of The Colby
Agency's J. T. Baxley and his bride, Eve Mattson.

That is, of course, if J.T. can find the woman who left him
at the altar. Considering he's a private investigator for one
of the top agencies in the country—the best of the best—
that shouldn't be a problem. The real setback is that his
bride isn't who she appears to be…and her mysterious
past has put them both in danger.

*Enjoy an exclusive glimpse of Debra Webb's
latest addition to*
THE COLBY AGENCY:
ELITE RECONNAISSANCE DIVISION

THE BRIDE'S SECRETS

*Available August 2009
from Harlequin Intrigue®.*

The dark figures on the dock were still firing. The bullets cutting through the surface of the water without the warning boom of shots told Eve they were using silencers.

That was to her benefit. Silencers decreased the accuracy of every shot and lessened the range.

She grabbed for the rocks. Scrambled through the darkness. Bumped her knee on a boulder. Cursed.

Burrowing into the waist-deep grass, she kept low and crawled forward. Faster. Pushed harder. Needed as much distance as possible.

Shots pinged on the rocks.

J.T. scrambled alongside her.

He was breathing hard.

They had to stay close to the ground until they reached the next row of warehouses. Even though she was relatively certain they were out of range at this point, she wasn't taking any risks. And she wasn't slowing down.

J.T. had to keep up.

The splat of a bullet hitting the ground next to Eve had her rolling left. Maybe they weren't completely out of range.

She bumped J.T. He grunted.

His injured arm. Dammit. She could apologize later.

Half a dozen more yards.

Almost in the clear.

As she reached the cover of the alley between the first two warehouses she tensed.

Silence.

No pings or splats.

She glanced back at the dock. Deserted.

Time to run.

Her car was parked another block down.

Pushing to her feet, she sprinted forward. The wet bag dragged at her shoulder. She ignored it.

By the time she reached the lot where her car was parked, she had dug the keys from her pocket and hit the fob. Six seconds later she was behind the wheel. She hit the ignition as J.T. collapsed into the passenger seat. Tires squealed as she spun out of the slot.

"What the hell did you do to me?"

From the corner of her eye she watched him shake his head in an attempt to clear it.

He would be pissed when she told him about the tranquilizer.

She'd needed him cooperative until she formulated a plan. A drug-induced state of unconsciousness had been the fastest and most efficient method to ensure his continued solidarity.

"I can't really talk right now." Eve weaved into the right lane as the street widened to four lanes. What she needed was traffic. It was Saturday night—shouldn't be that difficult to find as soon as they were out of the old warehouse district.

A glance in the rearview mirror warned that their unwanted company had caught up.

Sensing her tension, J.T. turned to peer over his left shoulder.

"I hope you have a plan B."

She shot him a look. "There's always plan G." Then she pulled the Glock out of her waistband.

Cutting the steering wheel left, she slid between two vehicles. Another veer to the right and she'd put several cars between hers and the enemy.

She was betting they wouldn't pull out the firepower in the

open like this, but a girl could never be too sure when it came to an unknown enemy.

Deep blending was the way to go.

Two traffic lights ahead the marquis of a movie theater provided exactly the opportunity she was looking for.

The digital numbers on the dash indicated it was just past midnight. Perfect timing. The late movie would be purging its audience into the crowd of teenagers who liked hanging out in the parking lot.

She took a hard right onto the property that sported a twelve-screen theater, numerous fast-food hot spots and a chain super-store. Speeding across the lot, she selected a lane of parking slots. Pulling in as close to the theater entrance as possible, she shut off the engine and reached for her door.

"Let's go."

Thankfully he didn't argue.

Rounding the hood of her car, she shoved the Glock into her bag, then wrapped her arm around J.T.'s and merged into the crowd.

With her free hand she finger-combed her long hair. It was soaked, as were her clothes. The kids she bumped into noticed, gave her death-ray glares.

They just didn't know.

As she and J.T. moved in closer to the building, she grabbed a baseball cap from an innocent bystander. The crowd made it easy. The kid who owned the cap had made it even easier by stuffing the cap bill-first into his waistband at the small of his back.

Pushing through the loitering crowd, she made her way to the side of the building next to the main entrance. She pushed J.T. against the wall and dropped her bag to the ground. Peeled off her tee and let it fall.

His gaze instantly zeroed in on her breasts, where the cami she wore had glued to her skin like an extra layer. A zing of desire shot through her veins.

Not the time.

With a flick of her wrist she twisted her hair up and clamped the cap atop the blonde mass.

"They're coming," J.T. muttered as he gazed at some point beyond her.

"Yeah, I know." She planted her palms against the wall on either side of him and leaned in. "Keep your eyes open. Let me know when they're inside."

Then she planted her lips on his.

* * * * *

Will J.T. and Eve be caught in the moment?
Or will Eve get the chance to reveal all of her secrets?
Find out in
THE BRIDE'S SECRETS
by Debra Webb
Available August 2009
from Harlequin Intrigue®

We'll be spotlighting a different series every month throughout 2009 to celebrate our 60th anniversary.

LOOK FOR
HARLEQUIN INTRIGUE®
IN AUGUST!

To commemorate the event, Harlequin Intrigue® is thrilled to invite you to the wedding of the Colby Agency's J.T. Baxley and his bride, Eve Mattson.

Look for *Colby Agency: Elite Reconnaissance*

THE BRIDE'S SECRETS
BY DEBRA WEBB

Available August 2009

Harlequin® Historical
Historical Romantic Adventure!

From *USA TODAY* bestselling author
Margaret Moore

THE VISCOUNT'S KISS

When Lord Bromwell meets a young woman on the mail coach to Bath, he has no idea she is Lady Eleanor Springford—until *after* they have shared a soul-searing kiss!

The nature-mad viscount isn't known for his spontaneous outbursts of romance—and the situation isn't helped by the fact that the woman he is falling for is fleeing a forced marriage....

The Viscount and the Runaway...

Available August 2009
wherever you buy books.

You're invited to join our Tell Harlequin Reader Panel!

By joining our new reader panel you will:

- Receive Harlequin® books—they are FREE and yours to keep with no obligation to purchase anything!
- Participate in fun online surveys
- Exchange opinions and ideas with women just like you
- Have a say in our new book ideas and help us publish the best in women's fiction

In addition, you will have a chance to win great prizes and receive special gifts! See Web site for details. Some conditions apply. Space is limited.

To join, visit us at

www.TellHarlequin.com.

REQUEST YOUR FREE BOOKS!
2 FREE NOVELS PLUS 2
FREE GIFTS!

HARLEQUIN *Romance*

From the Heart, For the Heart

YES! Please send me 2 FREE Harlequin® Romance novels and my 2 FREE gifts (gifts are worth about $10). After receiving them, if I don't wish to receive any more books, I can return the shipping statement marked "cancel". If I don't cancel, I will receive 4 brand-new novels every month and be billed just $3.84 per book in the U.S. or $4.24 per book in Canada. That's a savings of at least 15% off the cover price! It's quite a bargain! Shipping and handling is just 50¢ per book.* I understand that accepting the 2 free books and gifts places me under no obligation to buy anything. I can always return a shipment and cancel at any time. Even if I never buy another book, the two free books and gifts are mine to keep forever.

114 HDN EYU3   314 HDN EYKG

Name	(PLEASE PRINT)	
Address		Apt. #
City	State/Prov.	Zip/Postal Code

Signature (if under 18, a parent or guardian must sign)

Mail to the **Harlequin Reader Service:**
IN U.S.A.: P.O. Box 1867, Buffalo, NY 14240-1867
IN CANADA: P.O. Box 609, Fort Erie, Ontario L2A 5X3

Not valid to current subscribers of Harlequin Romance books.

**Are you a subscriber of Harlequin Romance books
and want to receive the larger-print edition?
Call 1-800-873-8635 today!**

* Terms and prices subject to change without notice. Prices do not include applicable taxes. Sales tax applicable in N.Y. Canadian residents will be charged applicable provincial taxes and GST. Offer not valid in Quebec. This offer is limited to one order per household. All orders subject to approval. Credit or debit balances in a customer's account(s) may be offset by any other outstanding balance owed by or to the customer. Please allow 4 to 6 weeks for delivery. Offer available while quantities last.

Your Privacy: Harlequin Books is committed to protecting your privacy. Our Privacy Policy is available online at www.eHarlequin.com or upon request from the Reader Service. From time to time we make our lists of customers available to reputable third parties who may have a product or service of interest to you. If you would prefer we not share your name and address, please check here. ☐

HR09R

Stay up-to-date on all your romance reading news!

The Inside Romance newsletter is a **FREE** quarterly newsletter highlighting our upcoming series releases and promotions!

Go to
eHarlequin.com/InsideRomance
or e-mail us at
InsideRomance@Harlequin.com
to sign up to receive
your **FREE** newsletter today!

Coming Next Month

Available August 11, 2009

**Have a holiday romance with Harlequin in August
and get swept away by our gorgeous, sun-kissed heroes!**

#4111 CATTLE BARON: NANNY NEEDED Margaret Way
Scandalously gate-crashing her ex-fiancé's wedding costs Amber her
job! Then brooding rancher Cal MacFarlane makes her nanny to his
baby nephew. Once the media frenzy dies down, can Cal convince
Amber to stay?

#4112 HIRED: CINDERELLA CHEF Myrna Mackenzie
After an accident that shattered her spine, Darcy's made a new life for
herself as a chef. Her most recent position might be temporary, but her
gorgeous boss has other ideas....

#4113 GREEK BOSS, DREAM PROPOSAL Barbara McMahon
Escape Around the World
Aboard his luxury yacht, Nikos isn't looking for love. But sharing the
breathtaking beauty of the idyllic Greek islands with his pretty new
employee is driving him crazy!

#4114 MISS MAPLE AND THE PLAYBOY Cara Colter
Primary-school teacher Beth Maple is cautious and conventional. Yet
when stand-in dad Ben appears at the school gates with his good looks
and confident swagger, Beth is starstruck!

#4115 BOARDROOM BABY SURPRISE Jackie Braun
Baby on Board
When pregnant Morgan arrives at billionaire Bryan's office looking for
her baby's father, two things become apparent: she has mistaken him for
his late brother, and she's in labor—in the boardroom!

#4116 BACHELOR DAD ON HER DOORSTEP Michelle Douglas
Jaz is back in her hometown, determined to face her old flame Connor
with dignity—and distance. But she hadn't reckoned on Connor being
even more irresistibly handsome—or a bachelor dad!